LOVE SOLVES THE PROBLEM

The dressing table, which was nearly three hundred years old, was a fine piece of furniture that any museum would be delighted to possess.

Sheila really hoped that her cousin would respect it and keep it where it had always been in the largest and most prestigious bedroom in the house.

At the same time she hated to think of the things that had been such a joy to her mother being sold.

Before she went back to her own bedroom, she took one last look round her mother's room.

She felt for a moment that she was still there in the four-poster bed with its beautiful curtains.

'Help me, Mama, help me,' she said silently in her heart. 'I am now all alone in the world and it is very very frightening. But somehow, wherever you are, I know that you will be thinking of me and keeping me safe from all that is wrong and evil.'

It was a prayer that came from the very depths of her soul.

With her eyes blinded with tears she ran from the room, closing the door behind her.

THE BARBARA CARTLAND
PINK COLLECTION

Titles in this series

LOVE SOLVES THE PROBLEM

BARBARA CARTLAND

Barbaracartland.com Ltd

ISBN 978-1-78213-568-5

Printed and bound in Great Britain
by Mimeo of Huntingdon, Cambridgeshire.

THE BARBARA CARTLAND PINK COLLECTION

Dame Barbara Cartland is still regarded as the most prolific bestselling author in the history of the world.

In her lifetime she was frequently in the Guinness Book of Records for writing more books than any other living author.

Her most amazing literary feat was to double her output from 10 books a year to over 20 books a year when she was 77 to meet the huge demand.

She went on writing continuously at this rate for 20 years and wrote her very last book at the age of 97, thus completing an incredible 400 books between the ages of 77 and 97.

Her publishers finally could not keep up with this phenomenal output, so at her death in 2000 she left behind an amazing 160 unpublished manuscripts, something that no other author has ever achieved.

Barbara's son, Ian McCorquodale, together with his daughter Iona, felt that it was their sacred duty to publish all these titles for Barbara's millions of admirers all over the world who so love her wonderful romances.

So in 2004 they started publishing the 160 brand new Barbara Cartlands as *The Barbara Cartland Pink Collection*, as Barbara's favourite colour was always pink – and yet more pink!

The Barbara Cartland Pink Collection is published monthly exclusively by Barbaracartland.com and the books are numbered in sequence from 1 to 160.

Enjoy receiving a brand new Barbara Cartland book each month by taking out an annual subscription to the Pink Collection, or purchase the books individually.

The Pink Collection is available from the Barbara Cartland website www.barbaracartland.com via mail order and through all good bookshops.

In addition Ian and Iona are proud to announce that The Barbara Cartland Pink Collection is now available in ebook format as from Valentine's Day 2011.

For more information, please contact us at:

Barbaracartland.com Ltd.
Camfield Place
Hatfield
Hertfordshire AL9 6JE
United Kingdom

Telephone: +44 (0)1707 642629
Fax: +44 (0)1707 663041
Email: info@barbaracartland.com

THE LATE DAME BARBARA CARTLAND

Barbara Cartland who sadly died in May 2000 at the age of nearly 99 was the world's most famous romantic novelist who wrote 723 books in her lifetime with worldwide sales of over 1 billion copies and her books were translated into 36 different languages.

As well as romantic novels, she wrote historical biographies, 6 autobiographies, theatrical plays, books of advice on life, love, vitamins and cookery. She also found time to be a political speaker and television and radio personality.

She wrote her first book at the age of 21 and this was called *Jigsaw*. It became an immediate bestseller and sold 100,000 copies in hardback and was translated into 6 different languages. She wrote continuously throughout her life, writing bestsellers for an astonishing 76 years. Her books have always been immensely popular in the United States, where in 1976 her current books were at numbers 1 & 2 in the B. Dalton bestsellers list, a feat never achieved before or since by any author.

Barbara Cartland became a legend in her own lifetime and will be best remembered for her wonderful romantic novels, so loved by her millions of readers throughout the world.

Her books will always be treasured for their moral message, her pure and innocent heroines, her good looking and dashing heroes and above all her belief that the power of love is more important than anything else in everyone's life.

*"I have always found that love can solve any problem
however intractable it might seem at the time. But then
what problem can possibly survive the God-given burning
intensity of real love between a man and a woman."*

Barbara Cartland

CHAPTER ONE
1855

"I am afraid, your Ladyship, I have bad news to tell you," the man said slowly as if every word was difficult for him.

Lady Sheila Rosswood gave a sigh and replied in a low voice,

"I was expecting it. You mean that my father has left no money at all."

"There are unfortunately," the man added, "a few debts, but I feel sure that they will be taken over by the new Earl to the estate."

Lady Sheila thought that this was doubtful, but she did not say so aloud.

She merely enquired,

"Is there anything left of my mother's money which she left to me in her will?"

The man, who was a senior banker from the local bank, then looked down at his papers and answered,

"I was rather afraid that your Ladyship might ask that question. The answer is that the money was spent by your father in his last desperate gamble that proved, just like so many of the others, to be completely and hopelessly unsuccessful."

Sheila sighed.

Then she rose from her chair and walked over to the window and stared with unseeing eyes at the neglected garden below her.

It seemed to her almost impossible that her father could have been quite so foolish as to risk everything he had in spurious 'get rich quick' Companies that inevitably failed, usually before they had been launched for more than six months.

He had been so certain that one or another of his schemes would, in his own words, 'be triumphant', that he continued to throw his money away even after his family and his friends begged him to be more cautious.

He had always, Sheila thought, looked on life as a bit of a joke.

The fact that he was growing poorer and poorer had merely made him take greater risks.

He then became even more careless in investing his money than he had been before.

And so now that he was dead, Sheila had to know exactly what her position was well before the new Earl of Rosswood arrived.

The Hall, which had been in the Rosswood family for five generations, was in a bad state of repair with rotten woodwork and even broken windows.

But it was undoubtedly a beautiful building and its contents, which were entailed, were extremely valuable.

It was very fortunate, as Lady Sheila was so aware, that her father had not been able to squander the family paintings and antique furniture in all his hopeless efforts to make himself a millionaire.

But, because he had been brought up since he was a small boy to believe that his family came first, he had not touched any of the fine paintings that hung on the walls of the house.

Nor the ancient silver that was the envy of a great number of other Earls who could not put on such a display.

They were therefore at a disadvantage when it came to boasting of what they owned.

It seemed incredible to Sheila that, having spent all her mother's money that was quite a considerable amount and everything that had been left to her by her mother's family, she was completely penniless.

She was now forced to rely on the kindness and generosity of the new Earl.

This situation was made even more difficult than it was already by the fact that her father had always disliked Thomas Ross and the reports on him from other relations had never been very much to his credit.

Sheila was thinking to herself that nothing could be more humiliating than to have to plead with him to support her in some way.

Although she had not met him in nearly ten years, she had always thought of him as being a grim and rather disagreeable man.

As she had been very young at the time, she might, of course, have been mistaken.

Yet she was almost sure that, as for years her father had deliberately ignored Thomas and avoided every chance of meeting him, he would hardly in the circumstances feel kindly towards her.

It also went against the grain in every possible way for her to have to ask anyone for money and especially so from a member of her own family.

Let alone a man who had been cold-shouldered by her father for so long.

Thomas had also, she understood, been particularly disliked by her mother.

Because she suddenly felt helpless, Sheila turned from the window to say to the man who had come from the bank,

"What can I do, Mr. Cole?"

It was, although she did not mean it to be, a cry for help.

The man who was middle-aged and of considerable standing in the banking world, looked at Sheila somewhat sadly before he was forced to say,

"I am afraid there is nothing that your Ladyship can do except ask the new Earl for his assistance."

It was with difficulty that Sheila prevented herself from crying out she would rather die than do that.

At the same time she was well aware that she was almost in the position of having to starve or plead on her knees for charity.

It seemed extraordinary that there were none of the older members of her family left.

As her mother came from the North of Scotland, she had never been in touch with her relatives as they were so far away.

Some of them had written to her when her mother died, but the Countess had never travelled back to her old home to visit those of her Clan who were still alive.

Now there were only half a dozen who actually remembered her.

When her mother had married the ninth Earl of Rosswood, as it had been a marriage of love, no one had been happier than the Earl and his wife when they first moved into the ancestral home.

A year later Sheila had been born.

It was perhaps when the Earl learnt that his wife was unable to have any more children and so he would not have an heir that had made him in some strange way wish to become a millionaire.

His father had been to all intents and purposes a rich man.

But the expense of keeping up the large estate and the ancestral home had cost more at that time than it ever had in previous generations.

He had added a Racecourse to the estate as well as a number of fine pictures to the Picture Gallery, which he had bought in other countries.

These, like everything else in the house, had been entailed onto future generations.

When she was old enough to realise what he had done, Sheila thought that it was because he had no son that he was determined that her husband, when she did marry, would not be able to take anything other than herself from the Rosswoods.

It was more than a little complicated.

At the same time Sheila had realised that her father had had a very strange outlook on life.

Because he had no son to inherit, he wanted to die leaving those relations who had followed him something to admire him for and to be exceedingly grateful for because he had been so shrewd.

It was this sort of desire to shine as the ninth Earl that had made him gamble his money away in what now seemed an almost incredible act of stupidity.

Equally Sheila now realised that she had to face the brutal facts.

One fact was that she was completely penniless unless the new Earl was as generous as the representative from the bank hoped that he would be.

'What can I do? What can I do?' she asked herself.

5

She realised only too well deep inside herself that there was no answer to what was actually a cry from the heart.

"I have put down, your Ladyship," the banker was saying, "every possible detail of where and on what your father invested his money. I thought I would give a copy of it to the new Earl when he arrives."

"I think that would be quite unnecessary," Sheila said coldly. "In fact I think that I will have to move from here and I have no intention of being an encumbrance that I am sure he would find me when he takes over."

Looking at her the banker thought she was so pretty that it would be a very hard-hearted man who could refuse her.

As he could not express this view aloud, he said,

"I think, if you will forgive me saying so, my Lady, it would be a mistake to do anything in a hurry. After all this is a very large house and I feel sure that the Earl will understand that you have to plan for your future in every way before you leave."

"Unfortunately I have no plans at present that are of any significance," Sheila replied. "As you doubtless know, my father had very few relations still alive and I have never been in touch with my mother's relations as they live in the very North of Scotland."

The banker thought it extraordinary for anyone of such standing as the previous Earl to have so few friends.

But he had heard it said that he was a very strange man, who seldom entertained and was living alone except for his daughter.

He spent a great deal of his time in London where according to gossip he made friends with only those people who were promoting new Companies that needed money to produce new inventions, which once they started invariably failed completely.

Those who had invested in them were, like the Earl, astonished that any product that seemed so brilliant at first should fail so completely.

At the same time, because there was an excitement about innovation, they were absolutely convinced that the next investment would be a triumph.

They and her father were throwing their money into what finally appeared to be a bottomless pit.

'How could Papa be so stupid?' Sheila had asked herself again and again in the darkness of the night.

He had been very discreet about what he was doing simply because he truly believed that when he won, as he had so firmly set out to do, everyone would be amazed at his brilliance.

They would have to congratulate him whether they approved or not of what he had done.

When Sheila looked down the long list that had been prepared for her of her father's endless losses, she had wondered how any man could be so foolish as to believe that Fate would suddenly turn his dreams into reality.

But he had gone on plunging and plunging, losing and losing, until it was only his death that had prevented him from what might have been an even worse Fate.

It struck the banker, when he saw the expression of despair on the pretty face of Lady Sheila, that there must be a number of men who would find her very attractive and the fact that she was penniless would not matter in the slightest.

He could understand that, as she had been shut up in this old house with its treasures from past centuries, her father had forgotten that she was young and beautiful.

And that she should be presented to the Society she belonged to in London.

It was impossible not to feel very sorry for her, but there was nothing he could do.

As he put the papers back into his briefcase, he was wondering what he could say that would give her some comfort and perhaps a little hope.

"Are you quite certain, Lady Sheila," he now asked, "that there are no members of your family anywhere in the country, who would welcome the opportunity of getting to know you better?"

He paused before he went on,

"After all you have been here all alone with your father for a large number of years and they surely must be anxious to entertain you now that he can no longer look after you."

Sheila smiled.

"It is a question several people have already asked me," she replied. "The Vicar was one and the doctor was another, but after my mother died, my father left me to run the house and the estate while he went to London to make his fortune."

She gave a little sigh.

"As you know, he failed utterly and it is only now that I begin to wonder why we have so few relatives and why they have never been to see us in the past years."

"Have you an answer to that?" the banker enquired.

"It is only a negative one like everything else," she answered. "The truth was that my father did not encourage his family to visit him. Now they have either died or have moved away to other parts of the country and even abroad. In fact I could hardly believe it when at his funeral there were no relatives at all to mourn for him."

She hesitated for a moment before she went on,

"The only people who came were friends from the County and those we employed."

She had wondered that after his death had appeared in the newspapers if anyone would come to the funeral or write a letter of condolence to her.

But nothing had happened and no one had turned up and Sheila was forced to face the fact that she not only had no money but no relatives.

She supposed that in a way it was her fault when she had left school at seventeen that she had not asked her friends to come and stay.

Nor had she forced her father to arrange some sort of party for them.

The last years she had been at school her mother had been ill and she had therefore been unable to invite her girlfriends to come to stay.

And after her mother had died, her father had spent almost all his time in London or in travelling around the country for business reasons.

Because she was perfectly happy riding her father's horses and reading as many books as she could in the huge library, it had never struck her for a single moment that she might need more sophisticated entertainment.

There were only the elderly servants who had been in the house for years, who did everything in their power to spoil her.

There were special dishes for her because the cook knew how much she enjoyed them.

There were abundant flowers from the garden.

Her two dogs who accompanied her everywhere she went were labradors and they gave, it seemed to her, every companionship she could possibly need.

One dog, Dickie, had moved now to stand beside her at the window and, when she then turned back into the room, he sat down by her side waiting for her to take him out into the garden or to the stables.

The other dog, Teal, was already sitting on the sofa waiting for her to sit down beside him.

As she did so, he moved his head towards her as she bent to caress the softness of his fur as she always did.

"What I would like to suggest to your Ladyship," the banker said, "is that you don't worry yourself too much over what I have told you this afternoon. Although it has to be faced sooner or later, I am sure that, when the new Earl arrives, you will find him only too anxious to accept your help as you helped your father in running the estate."

He paused before he added,

"After all there are enough bedrooms in this house for you to have no need to look for any more!"

He said the last words as if they were a joke, but Sheila did not smile.

"I will have to face the fact, Mr. Cole," she replied, "that this house no longer belongs to me. The new Earl may well have many friends he can fill the bedrooms with, which have been empty for far too long."

"I still think that he will need your assistance, Lady Sheila," the banker answered. "I do beg of you not to make plans to leave unless you have somewhere definite to go and people to look after you."

He smiled before he went on,

"You are still very young and there are many years in front of you in which you can enjoy yourself and forget that your father was so unsuccessful in his endeavours to become rich."

"Papa always believed that he would be successful one day and it is rather hard to face the fact that he not only failed, but he will not be remembered as he so wanted to be."

The banker knew this to be true and then, after a moment's rather uncomfortable pause, he said,

"Of course we would like to help your Ladyship in any way we possibly can."

"You have been very kind and very patient," Sheila said, "and I am exceedingly grateful. I have to be practical about my problems, as you would be if you were in the same position."

The banker thought to himself he would never be in the same position as the late Earl had been in when he died.

However, there was no point in him saying so and making things worse than they were already.

As he rose to his feet, he offered,

"If I can be of any assistance, Lady Sheila, I am only too willing to help and please feel free to contact me at any time."

"It is very kind of you, Mr. Cole," she replied.

She rose as she spoke from the sofa and Teal rose with her.

"I will, of course, let you know my new address when I have one. If by any chance any money does come in from any of my Papa's investments, would you be kind enough to let me know?"

"Of course I will," the banker said.

He knew, however, that it was almost impossible that anything would turn up in the future.

He could only say as he shook Sheila's hand,

"Once again I do beg of you not to do anything in a hurry. But stay here and wait to see if the new Earl needs you as much as your father did."

"You have been very kind and I can only thank you from the bottom of my heart for all your concern," Sheila replied.

She shook the banker's hand as she spoke.

As she walked to the door, she said,

"I expect that Wilkins will be in the hall to see you out."

As the banker walked down the passage to the hall, he was quite certain that Wilkins, who was the old butler, would be waiting for him.

He had guessed when he arrived that he had bad news for Lady Sheila and he had begged him to give it to her as kindly as he possibly could.

"I've been here for over forty years," Wilkins said, "but I've never known things to be quite so bad as I hears they be today."

"Very bad indeed," the banker had said. "I am just wondering if there are any relatives who will be offering a home to her Ladyship."

Wilkins shook his head.

"No one as I can think of," he replied. "The Missus and I be wondering where she can go and what she can do."

"There must be somebody," the banker said, "who would look after her. After all at her age she definitely needs a chaperone. It's just impossible for her to live alone here or anywhere else."

That's what I says to the Missus," Wilkins agreed. "But we can't think of anyone."

"Well, we can only hope that the new Earl will see where his duty lies," the banker replied.

The carriage he had come in from the bank, which was only five miles away in the town, was waiting for him outside.

He climbed into it and, as Wilkins closed the door after him, the driver started the horses.

The carriage moved slowly away down the drive and Wilkins watched it until it was almost out of sight.

With a sigh he walked back to the house and down the passage that led to the study where Sheila had received the banker.

As he opened the door, she turned from the window where she had been standing and asked,

"Has he gone, Wilkins?"

"He's driven away, my Lady, and I understands the only thing he brought for you today was gloom and more gloom."

"That is right, Wilkins. My position is even worse than it was before he arrived."

"Well then, all your Ladyship can do," Wilkins said consolingly, "is to wait until the new gentleman who takes your father's place arrives and see what he has to say."

"I am certain of one thing," Sheila said, "he will not want to have a young woman without a penny to her name on his hands. So the sooner I find somewhere to go the better."

"Now don't you talk like that, my Lady," Wilkins said. "You knows as well as I do that this be your home as much if not more than his. It be his duty as Head of the Family, what be left of it, to look after you and see that you are in no difficulties."

Sheila made a gesture with her hands.

"Why would he want to do that?" she asked. "After all Papa never liked him and made it clear what he felt. And we never asked him here. In fact I cannot remember seeing him after he came to Mama's funeral."

Wilkins had no answer to this.

He merely suggested,

"I'll fetch your tea for you, my Lady, and, as the Missus has cooked you a special cake, she will be very hurt if you don't eat several pieces of it."

Sheila smiled.

"You are both so kind to me," she sighed. "I am just wondering if I pretend to be a kitchen maid whether I could stay on here without the new Earl becoming aware of it."

Wilkins chuckled.

"I doubt if anyone would have your Ladyship for a kitchen maid however hard you tried. If you asks me, his Lordship, when he does arrive, will be askin' you to keep him company in the dining room."

Sheila thought that this was very unlikely, but she did not want to argue with Wilkins and merely said,

"It is kind of Mrs. Wilkins to make the sponge cake I always like. Tell her I will gobble up every bit of it."

"I knows that'll please her," Wilkins answered as he went to the door.

As he closed it behind him, Sheila walked again to the window.

The garden was not as well kept as it had been in her mother's time, for the simple reason that her father had been unable to pay the wages of the two gardeners, who in consequence had left.

But she thought that nothing could ever be more beautiful than the lawn with the large fountain throwing its water up into the sky.

There were a few flowers in beds on either side of the lawn and she could well remember when she was small being allowed to pick them for her mother.

This was her world.

The world that she believed she belonged to until Eternity.

Now it was no longer hers.

It was only a question of when and how she had to leave it.

'What shall I do? What can I do?' she repeatedly kept asking herself.

The question had been racing through her mind all day.

Each time she felt it grow and grow until it filled not only her brain and her body but the sky above and the earth below.

'What shall I do? What shall I do?' she heard it again and again.

And every time she felt as though there must be an answer.

Yet there was just silence until the words repeated themselves again.

Quite suddenly, almost as if the fountain and the birds in the trees were answering the question which had been echoing and re-echoing in her head since early in the morning, she knew that there was an answer.

What she had been to her father, had in a way been a secretary.

She had written the letters for him in her very neat writing because he himself wrote rather badly and he was always afraid that people would misunderstand what he was trying to say.

She had also, after her mother had died and there was no secretary in the house, written up the accounts and paid all the bills at the local shops as well as giving the servants their wages.

There had, of course, always been endless trouble in finding the money.

Sheila had been sure that on one or two occasions towards the end of his life her father had sold small items that were not that noticeable, although like everything else in the house they were entailed.

Looking back, she could remember when she had said to him,

"I must do the wages next Saturday, Papa. But they said when I last went to the bank that I was to tell that you there was no money in the household account."

"How stupid of me to forget it," her father had replied. "Of course I will see that you have some money. I am going to London tomorrow and I will bring you back what you need. How much do you want?"

By that time Sheila was paying not only the wages of the servants in the house but also those who worked in the garden and the grooms who looked after their very few horses.

When she told him the sum she required, her father had stared at her for a moment as if he could hardly believe that she wanted so much.

But he had said nothing and Sheila felt sure that he would bring her back what she required when he returned from London.

He had done so, but he had taken a suspiciously long time in the pantry when Wilkins had gone off to the village to purchase some food that his wife needed in the kitchen.

Rather stupidly, she thought later, Sheila had said to her father,

"What were you looking for in the pantry, Papa? Wilkins is only in the village for a short while and when he comes back he will find you anything you want."

"I was looking at some of the old family silver," her father had replied to her in a casual manner. "Most of it is stamped with our Crest, but some of it I noticed was not, which seems rather careless to me."

Sheila would not have thought any more about this particular conversation if three days later Wilkins had not said to her,

"Did his Lordship take any silver bowls with him when he went to London? I am sure that there were more of them at the back of the cupboard in the pantry than there are now."

Because Sheila had not wanted to make Wilkins suspicious in any way, she had said,

"He did say something about some of the silver not having the family Crest on it. If he took any with him to London, it would be because he thought that they should be stamped like the rest of the silver."

Wilkins had not queried her explanation.

Nor had he ever said, as he might well have done, that the bowls had not been returned.

It would have been too dangerous to sell one of the paintings, although they were incredibly valuable.

Just as some of the books in the library were first editions and talked about almost reverently by anyone who was interested in antique books.

It had seemed incredible both to her father and to Sheila that the library should have been included in the list of those items that were entailed and were inspected every three months by the diligent Trustees of the estate.

Yet Sheila was aware that, when her father wanted to invest in some new and exciting venture, anything which was saleable disappeared for some reason or another and never appeared again.

She was far too tactful to say anything to her father and far too loyal to mention it to the Trustees.

Occasionally they would point out that something was missing, but he invariably had a good excuse that the item in question was being mended or reframed.

Because there was so much to inspect, they would believe him when he said that the object was only away for a short time.

Now she wished that she herself had prevented her father from selling what had been hers and left to her by her mother.

"I want you to have all my jewellery, darling," her mother had said when she was ill. "When you wear my pearls and my diamonds, think of me."

"I am always thinking of you, Mama," Sheila had answered. "Don't talk as if you are leaving me because I need you so much."

She had known even as she spoke that the doctors had said that there was no hope for her mother.

The growing cancer in her body, for which there was no cure, was gradually increasing.

"Don't leave me, Mama," Sheila had begged her with tears in her eyes.

"I don't want to," her mother had answered. "But, if I do, then you must look after your father. He does many stupid things because he loves me and he wants to show me how clever he is. But you must never let him know how completely hopeless his ideas are."

She had sighed before she went on,

"You must never reproach him when he himself has to face the fact that his projects have failed."

"I will do exactly what you tell me, Mama," Sheila had promised.

But she had known, even as she was speaking, that her mother had no idea how desperately her father was disposing of everything that was saleable in the house.

As the Countess was unable to leave her bedroom for the last six months of her life, she had no idea how many pieces had disappeared from the drawing room or from the cupboards in the music room.

Because her father had been so anxious for money, Sheila was quite certain that if her mother had lived longer he would have defied those who inspected the house every three months.

He would have sold paintings or anything else that would bring him money for his wild dream of becoming a millionaire.

As it was everything had gone.

Sheila was not even left with her mother's diamond necklace, which she had always loved more than any other of her jewels.

'It's no use looking back,' she told herself. 'I must now look forward. I must learn that at twenty-one I am perfectly capable of looking after myself and I must not rely on anyone to look after me.'

All the same it was very frightening.

She had never been on her own, but had always, except when she was at school, been at home in her own bedroom.

She had been happy to ride her father's horses and to walk in the beautiful garden and estate which encircled the house.

It was home.

The real home she loved.

But now it was no longer hers.

It belonged to a strange man who would take her father's place and have no further use for her.

'What can I do?' she asked herself again. 'What can I do to persuade him that I could be very useful if I stayed here? Even if I had to move into one of the cottages on the estate, I would be quite happy.'

As she spoke, her hand went out towards one of her dogs and he rubbed himself against her leg.

"I will look after you," she told him. "I will know then that I am not completely alone, but have you to love me as I love you."

She crouched down and then put her arms around Dickie's neck.

Despite all her efforts she now found herself crying because she was so afraid.

It was then, as she wiped away the tears from her eyes, that she heard a sound outside in the hall.

She wondered who it could be.

She thought that perhaps the man from the bank had returned having left something behind.

Then she heard Wilkins voice speaking, although she could not hear what he said.

Finally she was aware that two men were walking towards the study where she was with the dogs.

Wiping away her tears, she went to the window to stand looking out at the fountain.

She felt that they would not notice anything except what they had come to find.

Then, as the door opened, she heard Wilkins say in his most stentorian voice in which he invariably announced visitors,

"The Earl of Rosswood, my Lady."

Sheila turned from the window.

Coming into the room was the man she had vaguely remembered seeing years ago.

Yet she knew that she would have recognised him if they had met without any introduction.

She had always thought that there was something rather grim and in a way impersonal about him.

This feeling seemed to have deepened and grown stronger with the years that had passed.

The new Earl's hair was certainly grey where it had been dark and there were lines on his face that had not been there when she had last seen him.

Yet even as she thought of him being somewhat unpleasant when they had first met, she knew now as he walked towards her that this had increased over the years rather than faded.

"Good afternoon, Sheila," the Earl began. "I expect you are surprised to see me and I should have let you know that I was arriving. But I only learnt of your father's death a week ago when I was in Spain. Therefore I could not be at the funeral and it has taken me all this time to return to England."

Sheila held out her hand to him as he spoke.

When he took it, she thought that his hand was cold and hard.

"I am sorry you could not be at Papa's funeral." Sheila said politely.

"Would you like tea, my Lord," Wilkins asked, "or would you prefer something stronger?"

"What is there?" the Earl asked him, taking his hand from Sheila's as he spoke.

"There's a bottle of champagne in the cellar, my Lord, which was a present to her Ladyship. There also be some bottles of white wine which his late Lordship, God rest his soul, never liked."

The new Earl thought for a moment.

Then he said,

"Bring up a bottle of the white wine and I will have the champagne with my dinner."

"Very good, my Lord," Wilkins said and then left the room.

The Earl looked round and said to Sheila,

"I suppose you are staying here. I was wondering whether I would find the house empty."

"I am staying," Sheila said in a very small voice, "because I have nowhere to go and I was hoping perhaps you would give me a little time to look round before you asked me to leave."

The Earl looked at her as if he was surprised before he answered,

"I had imagined that you would be with one of the family. After all you can hardly expect to stay here now it is no longer yours, but mine."

"I am afraid there are no members of the family left," Sheila replied. "Not my father's family at any rate and I have never met those of my mother's because they live so far away from here."

The Earl stared at her.

"Are you telling me," he asked, "that you expect to stay here now that I have taken it over?"

"I had certainly hoped that perhaps you would find me somewhere to go," Sheila replied.

The Earl walked across to the window and stood gazing out at the garden.

"I can see no reason," he said, "why your father, who paid very little attention to me, should expect me to provide you with accommodation or funding."

"Papa has left no money as I expect you will have heard," Sheila pointed out. "In fact, to be frank, he died heavily in debt. Therefore, not having a single penny to my name, I have nowhere to go and no chance of looking after myself without help."

The Earl turned from the window to look at her with astonishment.

"Are things as bad as that?" he asked. "It does not surprise me, as your father was exceedingly stupid where money was concerned. I quite expected the house to be in the crumbling state I noticed as I came up the drive."

"It's not as bad as that," Sheila replied. "But we have had to dispense with one or two of the men simply because we could not afford to pay them."

"Your father must have known that this was likely to happen," the Earl said, "when he threw money away in what one can only describe as the way of a madman."

Sheila stiffened.

"I don't think," she protested, "it is correct of you to speak of my father like that. He wanted the money not for himself but for the house and for the estate. If he was unfortunate, one cannot blame him for going on trying."

The Earl laughed and it was not a pleasant sound.

"That is one way of putting it," he said. "But from all I have heard, your father was foolhardy in the way he handled money and the result is that you are looking to me to provide for you, which was his business and not mine."

Sheila pulled herself up.

"I will leave tomorrow morning," she replied. "It is too late now for me to travel anywhere and I am sure you will not deny me a bed for the night and time to collect my belongings."

"Take what you like if they belong to you," the Earl retorted. "But let me make it perfectly clear that I have no intention of making up for your father's stupidity."

He paused before he continued,

"As you are well aware, it would be quite wrong for you to stay here now that you no longer can call the house your own. Therefore I can only hope that you will find other accommodation as quickly as possible."

As he spoke, there was a glint in his eye which told Sheila without words that he was paying her back for the way he had been treated, or thought that he had been, by her father in the past.

He had expected this to happen when he arrived and so he had been prepared to throw her out even before he had arrived here.

Holding her head high and moving across the room slowly, Sheila reached the door.

Turning round she said,

"You have made yourself very clear, my Lord. I can only hope that you will find things as much in order as it has been possible to put them. As you have suggested, I will leave tomorrow as soon as I can make arrangements to do so."

She did not wait for the Earl to answer, but went out of the room closing the door very quietly behind her.

Wilkins was waiting for her in the passage.

As she walked up to him, she said before he could speak,

"I am to leave as quickly as possible. Where can I go? Oh, Wilkins, tell me where I can go?"

She was looking up at him as she spoke.

There was a note of fear in her voice that the butler had never heard before.

CHAPTER TWO

"I thought that this would happen," Wilkins said. "Now you come along with me, my Lady, and I'll tell you what I've been plannin'."

Sheila looked at him in surprise.

However, as he was moving to the doorway under the staircase that led to the kitchen, she followed him.

They walked along the corridor which she had run along when she was only a child to ask the cook for some delicious titbit that could only be found in the kitchen.

She was thinking with an irrepressible fear that she might never see her home again.

After she left tomorrow morning she did not know where she would lay her head tomorrow night.

They found that Mrs. Wilkins was working in the kitchen preparing luncheon.

As she walked in with Wilkins, she raised her head and looked at her questioningly.

"It be just as I had expected," Wilkins said. "Her Ladyship's been turned out and she's nowhere to go."

Mrs. Wilkins drew in her breath.

"I've never heard of anythin' so disgraceful," she said. "But it be what we all knew his new Lordship'd be like and he's not wasted much time in showin' us what he is."

Sheila did not answer.

She merely sat down in a chair beside the table and looked at Wilkins with a plea for help in her eyes that no one could possibly miss.

To her surprise he sat down at the table beside her and said,

"The Missus and I were certain this would happen after all we'd heard about his new Lordship. So we've been makin' plans during the last few months so as to be ready for it."

"I don't understand," Sheila murmured.

"Well, it be like this," Wilkins said. "We says to ourselves, we says, that when his Lordship comes, from what we've heard of him, he'll not be wantin' anyone as pretty and clever as you be to run the house and look after him."

"That is true enough," Sheila sighed.

"So I says to meself long before your father dies," Wilkins went on, "that we now has to think of you and do somethin' to keep you from bein' thrown out of the only home you've ever had."

Sheila was listening to him intently.

She did not say anything and so Wilkins continued,

"I knows that your father were up to no good long before he faced the fact himself that everythin' he thought would bring him millions only made him poorer than he was afore he'd heard of it."

"He thought that just one success would bring him what he needed," Sheila said as if she felt that she must stand up for her father in some way.

"Well, my guess then was that he was makin' one mistake after another," Wilkins replied. "So I says to the Missus we has to do somethin'."

"He was very firm about it," Mrs. Wilkins chipped in. "Although I said it were not our business, we both felt we loved you too much, my Lady, to let you sink into the mud, so to speak."

"It was kind of you to think of me," Sheila just managed to say, as she could feel tears beginning to well up in her eyes.

"I knows your father was lookin' for somethin' he could sell," Wilkins said, "to put into one of them fancy Companies that always went bust."

He paused before he added,

"So I hid one or two things, which I knew he would sell if he found them."

"What things?" Sheila asked.

"Well, I didn't take too much," Wilkins responded, "because he might have accused me of stealin', but the ones I show you now will all bring in a few pennies to keep you alive."

He got up from the table as he spoke and went to a drawer in the dresser.

He pulled out an apron and some cloths and threw them on the floor.

Then he brought out an odd collection of silver and gold, which Sheila looked at with surprise.

She recognised one or two of the pieces as being part of a larger collection and some that she did not even recall.

Some of them had a pattern on them while some were inset with precious stones.

There were several candlesticks that she knew were very old and which would be appreciated by connoisseurs.

There were three inkpots that she knew he must have taken from the sitting rooms as they were of gold or silver. All were old enough to be collectors' pieces.

"You took these for me?" she questioned when she realised that Wilkins was watching her while she examined each one.

"They'll all bring in a pretty penny right enough," Wilkins said. "But, if your father'd had them, they'd be down the gutter by now."

"Poor Papa, he tried so hard," Sheila whispered.

"Well, he's got away without sufferin' for it," Mrs. Wilkins said, "and it's you who'll have to bear the burden of his foolish search for gold where there be none."

There was a sharp note in her voice.

But Sheila looked at her before she said,

"Whatever Papa did, he did it to keep this house going and to fill it as it used to be in his father's time with a large staff to keep it in perfect condition."

Mrs. Wilkins sighed.

"Of course that's what he meant to do, my dear."

"He sold everything he could," Sheila said almost beneath her breath. "But – you saved these for me?"

"Then they'll keep you goin' for a while," Wilkins replied. "Now you must plan who you'll go to and what you'll do."

"The answer to your first question is very easy," Sheila answered. "I have no relations in this part of the world. There are a few distant cousins left, but they live in the North of Scotland."

She hesitated before she went on,

"I have not heard from them for years and I doubt if they would be very pleased to see me – even if I could get there."

There was silence after she had spoken.

Then Wilkins piped up again,

"I've got an idea, but you may not like it."

"Tell me what it is?" Sheila asked him.

Wilkins paused for a moment.

She knew that he was feeling uncomfortable and she wondered why.

"Well, it be like this, my Lady," he said finally. "If you has no money, you has to become like us and then earn some."

"I agree with you," Sheila told him. "But what can I do? Who would have me in their business, if they have one, considering I know nothing except running this house and, of course, the estate when Papa was too busy or ill to worry about it."

"That's just what I was thinkin'," Wilkins replied. "That's why if you're goin' to take a job to keep yourself alive if nothin' else, that's what you can do."

Sheila stared at him.

"What do you mean?" she asked.

"Well, you did for his Lordship everythin' a good secretary would have done. I often says to the Missus, I says, 'that girl's got so many brains in her head she ought to be runnin' this house, then it'd be as smart as it ought to be and all the money would not be goin' down the drain elsewhere."

There was silence.

Then Sheila asked Wilkins,

"Are you suggesting I should apply for a position as a secretary?"

"Well, it ain't such a bad job as I sees it," Wilkins replied. "You don't want to be in the kitchen and you can't afford to sit in the dining room, so why not be like the secretary we had in the past who kept herself to herself.

We was respectful to her, especially when she paid us our money on Saturdays!"

Sheila laughed.

"I never thought of that. But, of course, I wrote all Mama's letters for her and even Papa's at the end when he had difficulty in seeing."

"And you did it extremely well and you kept the gardeners workin' even when they weren't paid," Wilkins told her.

Sheila laughed again.

"You make it sound very easy, but we have to find someone who wants to employ a secretary and, if you ask me they would much prefer a man to run a place as big as this."

"That goes without sayin'," Wilkins agreed. "At the same time there'd be men like your father who would find it easier to talk to a woman than to a man."

He stopped for a moment before he went on,

"In fact I remember him sayin' to me once a long time ago, 'that girl of mine, Wilkins, is far better at writin' letters and keepin' everything goin' than Mr. Martin ever was'."

Sheila smiled.

"I remember Mr. Martin. He was very precise and Mama found him rather a bore. But then he did what was expected of him and I always understood that he did it very well."

"He might have been worse," Wilkins said. "But I often think how fortunate she was to have you and your mother could never have done without you when she was too ill to write a letter herself."

Sheila knew that this was true.

She thought that Wilkins was being very sensible in realising that it was the one job she was really proficient at.

She had sometimes thought that, if they were really so poor they could not go on living at the house, she would like to work in a stable because she loved horses.

But she knew that there was no question of anyone wanting to employ her to do such a job because she was a woman.

It was always men who were employed as grooms and they would laugh at the idea of her pretending to be one.

Aloud she said,

"I am sure, Wilkins, you are right in thinking that the one thing I can do is to be a secretary. But I would have to find someone who wanted one and it is obvious to me that most people would prefer a man."

"That's where gentlemen be concerned," he replied. "But I suspect that your mother, if you had not been here would have employed a woman to write her letters."

He smiled before he went on,

"A lot of ladies would feel a bit uncomfortable if they were in bed and there was a man, who after all was only a senior servant, sittin' down next to them."

"You have an answer to everything," Sheila said. "I am very very grateful to you for thinking of me. But I feel I should not take all these precious pieces for myself, but give you some just in case my cousin refuses to employ you."

"I have fixed that already," Wilkins informed her. "He asks me when he arrived if I'd be prepared to stay on and, of course, he still wants the Missus in the kitchen."

"He would certainly not want to lose her," Sheila answered. "I only hope he gives you both the wages that Papa was unable to pay you towards the end."

31

She felt embarrassed as she said the words knowing how uncomfortable it had been that her father had thrown away the last of his money.

Not only because it affected her but also Wilkins and his wife.

One by one the other servants had left.

The housemaids, the under-housemaids and all the kitchen help. They all disappeared because they could not be paid.

Yet her father still went on believing that it was only a question of time before he won the mythical battle he was fighting.

Then the house and the estate would be restored to how it had been for hundreds of years.

"Now what I am going to suggest," Wilkins said, breaking what had been a rather poignant silence.

As Sheila gazed at him, he continued,

"I thinks, my Lady, you and I must go to London."

"Now I was just wondering," Sheila said, "where I should go. In fact I thought the only thing for me would be to go into the village and see if anyone would let me stay with them. Perhaps I could try to cook like Mrs. Wilkins or look after children."

There was silence for a moment.

Then Wilkins said,

"I really thinks, if you ask me, they would feel a bit uncomfortable seein' as you come from the Big House and has a title like your father. They always looked on you as bein' someone special, someone they could touch their cap to."

"I am afraid that no one will do that to me in the future," Sheila replied gloomily.

"Oh, yes they will!" Wilkins exclaimed. "I'll not have you givin' up, so there! If I takes you to London, we can stay at the old house which is where you ought to be dancing as a *debutante* night after night."

"The old house?" Sheila questioned. "How can we possibly go there? It was sold to one of Papa's friends, who he always said cheated him and when they met they pretended not to see each other."

Wilkins laughed.

"That might have been your father's way of goin' on, my Lady, but I had different ideas."

"What were they?" Sheila asked him.

"Well, first of all I makes friends with the cook, who always gave me somethin' special when your father and I stayed there and later with the butler, who I found a jolly chap. Havin' seen the house years ago when it were lookin' its best, we were real sorry that we were sinkin', so to speak, into the mire."

Sheila wondered how this concerned her.

But she had known ever since she was small that Wilkins was long-winded in what he had to say and it was best not to interrupt him.

She therefore waited until he continued his story,

"The last words, Newman, for that were the name of the butler, said to me before I leaves and that were a year or two ago were, 'if you ever comes to London, you can stay here whether they knows about it or not and I'll be real pleased to see you'."

Sheila gave a little gasp.

"So you can stay at the house in Park Lane and you think I could stay there too?"

"We won't have to pay," he replied, "and, unless things have altered, the food in the kitchen is as good as the food you get in the dining room."

Sheila laughed.

"When we reach London," she asked, "what are we going to do?"

"Well, firstly," Wilkins replied, "we'll sell these things. That'll be after I've left you with my friend in Park Lane. If they thinks it's just a lady wantin' a bit extra to powder her face, they'll not give you the same as they'll give me if they thinks I'm a real rogue who's stolen them."

Sheila smiled.

"Is it really as bad as that, Wilkins?"

"As far as you are concerned, my Lady, you wants every penny you can get and that's what I intends to get for you."

"Thank you, thank you so very much," Sheila said. "Do you think your friend at the house we used to have will know anyone who wants a secretary?"

Wilkins grinned.

"I knows the answer to that," he said. "You goes to Foxton's Agency and you will find out what they has on their books."

"Of course you are right, I did not think of that!" Sheila exclaimed. "Mama always used to go there when she wanted a lady's maid or a particularly good housemaid. But I had forgotten about them until now."

"That's where we got our servants from in the past for the house in London," Wilkins told her. "But you were only a child when we had that on our hands. Now it be gone like everything else."

He paused before he said,

"One thing after another until as you know there be nothing left except the things your father were scared to sell because it would have been illegal."

"I was so afraid that he would get into trouble with the Trustees," Sheila replied. "I am sure that, if they saw these items you have kept for me, they would say I had no right to them."

"Thems as ask no questions hears no lies," Wilkins answered. "Heaven knows there be little enough you be gettin' from the house that has always been your home."

"There's one thing you've forgotten," Mrs. Wilkins piped up.

"Oh yes!" Wilkins exclaimed. "I'd really forgotten about that."

He went to the drawer in the dresser.

Reaching to the back of it, he drew out what looked like a small parcel.

He undid it and inside there was a small leather box.

When he opened it, Sheila saw that it contained a ring, which she vaguely recognised as being worn by her mother in the past.

"How did you get that?" she asked. "I thought that Papa had taken all Mama's jewellery. I cried when he sold it all, but he said that he would buy some of it back when the Company he was investing in made millions of pounds as he was so sure that it would do."

"They always told your father all that nonsense, but I wanted to keep somethin' for you and your father never noticed that this was missin' when he sold your mother's pearls and the bracelets she loved after she passed on."

"But surely Papa must have been aware that it was missing?" Sheila asked.

"When I knew what your father was doin' and what silver had gone would never return," he said, "I thinks I should save somethin'. I was sure after your mother died it would be her jewels he would sell."

"So you kept this ring for me," Sheila murmured. "It is very very kind of you."

"Your father asked me what had happened to it," Wilkins continued, "but I tells him there was a stone loose and you'd sent it to the jewellers. Just by luck he then forgot all about it."

He scratched his head before he went on,

"As I never mentioned it again, it didn't go like the rest of your mother's jewels – down the drain."

Sheila gave a deep sigh.

But she did not speak and after a moment Wilkins carried on,

"Now you keep it safe, so that it's there when you really needs it, as I said to the Missus and she'll tell you it's the truth, her Ladyship must have somethin' to save her when things become so bad she has nowhere left to put her head."

"You are both very kind," Sheila replied. "I cannot tell you how glad I am that you are here to help me. I had no idea where I could go but, as Cousin Thomas has turned me out, I would have to leave here whether I wanted to or not."

"Well then, we'll go to London first thing in the mornin'," Wilkins declared. "The Missus'll look after him until I gets back. But I won't leave you until I knows you has somewhere to go."

"You are kind – so very kind," Sheila answered. "I know Mama would thank you if she was alive and indeed so would Papa."

She gave a deep sigh before she added,

"He really and truly believed that one day he would make his fortune in a big way, in which case everyone who had stood by him would have benefitted too and both of you especially."

She spoke in a way that was very moving.

Mrs. Wilkins wiped her eyes before she said,

"There, my Lady, you have always been someone who Wilkins and I admire. You were that brave when your mother died and have been braver still when your father followed her."

She looked across at her husband before she went on,

"We've often said to each other that you be like the child we never had and so we must look after you one way or another."

"It is what you are doing and you have no idea how grateful I am," Sheila told her.

She hesitated before she continued,

"I would be incredibly frightened – if I had to go to London alone and find some work to do."

"I'll tell the boys that we will be takin' the carriage drawn by two of the best horses left in the stable and we're goin' to London," Wilkins said.

He almost looked excited as he went on,

"We'll be off at six o'clock before his Lordship wakes up and tells us it's somethin' we're not to do."

"Do you really think we can borrow them without asking his permission?" Sheila asked.

"And have him say 'no'?" Wilkins said quizzically. "Not likely! We'll go off to London afore he's awake and with any luck he won't know we've gone. If he does, I'll just say I had to take you to London safely seein' as you had no other way of goin' as you had no money."

"It be disgraceful, really disgraceful," Mrs. Wilkins exclaimed, "turning you out like that! You hardly had time to breathe, let alone find someone to have you."

"I expect he guessed that there is no one who would want me," Sheila answered. "But I do feel sure that with your husband's help – I can find someone who will take me in."

She paused for a moment before she added,

"And thank you more than I can ever say for saving these things for me, so that at least I will have some money and will not have to beg in the streets like a pauper or die of starvation."

"We'll not have you doin' that," Mrs. Wilkins said, "as long as Wilkins and I have somewhere to put our own heads. If you asks me, you're too young and too pretty to go gallivantin' about the place. If Wilkins had listened to me, which he *never* does, I would have hidden you here in the back of the house – "

"But I told her," Wilkins interrupted, "that, if his Lordship had found you, we'd have been out too and I've no wish to be lookin' for another job when I've had this one for nigh on thirty-five years."

"Have you really been here as long as that?" Sheila asked. "To me you are part of this house, its history and everything else. I could not imagine it without you both."

"That's what I likes to hear," Wilkins said. "You can be sure that we'll do whatever we can for you."

"Thank you, thank – you!" Sheila cried.

Her voice broke on the words because she was so touched at their kindness in what she felt for a moment was a frightening and empty world where she was utterly and totally alone.

As she went upstairs to her bedroom, she thought it would be the last time that she would ever sleep in one of the State bedrooms.

The one that she was in was dedicated to Princess Mary who had slept there when she was only a girl.

Her mother's room, which was the most important in the whole house, had been honoured by having Queen Elizabeth as a guest when she had only just ascended the throne.

"Now pack everythin' you own and anythin' you think will be useful," Wilkins told her. "I've brought down all the luggage I thinks you'll need from the attic. But, if you still want more, I can fetch it first thing in the mornin' before we sets off for London."

Looking at the large number of trunks and boxes that seemed to fill her room, Sheila felt that she would not have enough clothes for them all.

After Wilkins had bid her goodnight and she was alone, she went into her mother's room.

She thought that she would be wise to take what clothes she could from what were still hanging in the large wardrobe after the Countess's death.

There was a fur coat that Sheila thought she would certainly be able to sell if, by the time the winter came, she had no money.

But the other clothes that were in perfect condition would, she knew, be useful to her.

Even if she earned sufficient money, which she was frightened she might not do, she would not have to buy clothes to keep herself from being cold even if she had to buy enough food to keep herself from being hungry.

There were one or two beautiful evening gowns which Sheila thought, although they might seem rather old for her, would certainly make her appear distinguished at any evening party she was invited to.

Then she laughed at the idea.

Who was going to ask her, a mere secretary, to the sort of parties her mother had enjoyed when she was first married to her father?

She had often been told how glamorous they were and how beautifully dressed the ladies had been and how they had danced to the most fashionable bands in the whole of London.

'I will not be needing these dresses,' Sheila said to herself as she looked at the beautiful embroidery on one of them and the exquisite lace on another.

She gave a sigh.

'But I don't want anyone else to wear them,' she went on, 'so they will be safe with me and that is what I know Mama would want them to be.'

Most of the dresses were practical and there were shoes that luckily fitted her, also a selection of hats which she put into two of the hat boxes.

It was after one o'clock when Sheila had finished packing.

But there were still some things she had to leave behind.

She thought perhaps that Mrs. Wilkins could hide them away in the attics so that the new Earl could not destroy them or give them away.

He would be unable to sell them, Sheila thought with a faint smile and anyone who wore them would look strange.

She hated to leave anything of her mother's behind, but everything of any value had already been sold.

Although she searched diligently, as she had done before in the drawers and wardrobes, there was, now she had packed, nothing left that anyone could use.

She just could not bear to think of anyone like her cousin handling or touching her beloved mother's clothes.

She was determined that when he went to look at the wardrobes and chest of drawers she had used, the new Earl would find nothing of any particular interest.

She only wished that she was able to take away the beautiful dressing table that had framed her mother's face when she did her hair.

There were little gold cupids walking around the mirror and the tall candlesticks that graced it were of gold angels climbing up to form a platform at the top.

She had always loved them ever since she was a child and now she hated to leave them behind.

But she realised that her father had not sold them, although they could have brought in a considerable amount of money, simply because he respected his wife even after she was dead.

The dressing table, which was nearly three hundred years old, was a fine piece of furniture that any museum would be delighted to possess.

Sheila really hoped that her cousin would respect it and keep it where it had always been in the largest and most prestigious bedroom in the house.

At the same time she hated to think of the things that had been such a joy to her mother being sold.

Before she went back to her own bedroom, she took one last look round her mother's room.

She felt for a moment that she was still there in the four-poster bed with its beautiful curtains.

'Help me, Mama, help me,' she said silently in her heart. 'I am now all alone in the world and it is very very frightening. But somehow, wherever you are, I know that you will be thinking of me and keeping me safe from all that is wrong and evil.'

It was a prayer that came from the very depths of her soul.

With her eyes blinded with tears she ran from the room, closing the door behind her.

CHAPTER THREE

Sheila and Wilkins left the next morning just before six o'clock.

When she had walked to the stables, she found him already there.

With the help of a sleepy stable boy, he had taken the two best horses left, put them into their harnesses and attached them to the open chaise that had been her father's joy and delight.

As they set off briskly down the drive, Sheila was wondering if she would ever see her home again and if she would ever find anywhere so hauntingly beautiful.

To the last question she knew that the answer was 'no'.

It would certainly not be anywhere she loved as she had loved her own home and garden ever since she could remember.

They had driven on silently for almost two miles before Wilkins suggested,

"I think we should stop for breakfast at one of the more obscure inns. It be no use us drivin' on and on on an empty stomach and we still has a long way to go."

"Yes, of course," Sheila agreed. "I reckon you are thinking of stopping at *The Oaks Restaurant* which is not very far away."

Wilkins laughed.

"I guessed you would remember it, my Lady," he replied. "Your father always stopped there either on his way out huntin' or on his way back. If anyone mourned your father's death in this part of the world, it were Mr. Ansell."

Mr. Ansell was an elderly man with white hair, who had set up a small inn some twenty years ago.

People stopped there for a meal out of kindness to its owner and the fact that it was a convenient place to tie up their horses while they were eating.

There were, however, only two other men there this morning when Sheila and Wilkins walked into the dining room.

"You must excuse me, my Lady, if I seem to be a bit over-familiar on this journey," Wilkins ventured to say, "but it's most important that no one in the County and certainly in London, should know that you are travellin' and livin' alone."

"You are quite right, Wilkins," Sheila replied, "and I am very grateful to you for looking after me. I have a feeling that I will be very bad at looking after myself."

"Now if things go wrong, my Lady, and you're in any trouble, just you come to me. The house is so big that his Lordship need not be aware you are with us especially if you keep with my wife and me in the kitchen."

Sheila thought that this was true.

But she wondered if she was being rather stupid at being thrown out of the house by the new Earl, when she might have hidden from him and remained safe and secure in her own home.

Then she told herself that she had to be brave and face the world as it was.

It was ridiculous when she was nearly twenty-one to think that she had to be cosseted and looked after as if she was a baby in arms.

'I will be all right,' she determined firmly.

At the same time something within her seemed to sink lower and lower at the thought of losing Wilkins.

When they had finished their meal and thanked the old publican for it, they drove on.

Actually they had reached the outskirts of London by ten o'clock.

And now there was traffic in the streets and there seemed to Sheila to be an army of people moving up and down the pavements.

It was so long since she had been to London that she had almost forgotten what their house in Park Lane looked like.

When she saw it again, she knew that when she had stayed there with her mother and father it had seemed full of adventure and excitement, even though they entertained very little.

She remembered leaning out of the window to gaze at the bustling scene of horses and carriages moving down Park Lane.

She used to sit and watch the children playing in Hyde Park on the other side of the road. It had all seemed rather like a theatre that she enjoyed, but was not quite real because she was not actually a part of it.

Now she was grown up and the house looked very much the same but somewhat older.

It seemed to her to have lost the enchantment she had always felt when she entered it as a small girl.

She certainly entered it now in a different way from how she had in the past.

Wilkins turned directly into the Mews at the back of the house.

There was an empty stall into which Sheila helped him put the two horses.

There seemed to be no one about, but they found food for them and fresh water. There was also enough clean straw in the stalls for them to lie down in comfort.

Having hung the bridles and harnesses up on hooks, Sheila realised what she had forgotten.

It was that three stalls in the Mews belonged to the house that had once been her father's and so there would be plenty of room for the owner's horses.

What was most important was not to be noticed or questioned by any of the servants.

She therefore hurried with Wilkins in through the garden at the back of the house and down the steps that led into the kitchen.

His good friend, Newman, the butler to the new owner of the house, greeted him with enthusiasm.

"It really cheers me up to see you after so long," Newman said. "What have you been doin' to keep away from us when you knows how welcome you be here. At least you know the way after all the years you lived here."

"I not only knows the way," Wilkins replied, "but I brought with me a friend who wants your help and your advice."

He laughed before he added,

"After all you've been livin' here in London where things happen, while I've been buried in the country."

They both chuckled at that.

Newman's wife, who was the cook, then started to prepare eggs, bacon and coffee for them.

They sat down at one end of the kitchen table while she cooked on the stove at the other end.

"Now tell me," Newman said to Wilkins, "why you are here and why you've brought this pretty young lady to London?"

"Trust you to get to the point right away," Wilkins replied. "This young lady – and I'm not going to tell you her name because we has to think of a new one for her – wants a job. So I am lookin' to you, Newman, to find her one."

Newman spread out his hands in despair.

"The new owner of the house counts his coins as if they be diamonds," he said. "My wife asked for more help in the kitchen three months ago and she's still havin' to cope with a lazy boy who only turns up when there be a party."

"We were not exactly thinkin' of the lady helpin' in the kitchen," Wilkins replied, "but she be a really excellent secretary and that's what she's been doin' with us in the country."

"That'll be a different thing all together," Newman answered. "You'll have to go to the Agency and find out what Mrs. Foxton has on her books."

He gave a deep sigh and went on,

"In the old days it were so easy. I only had to lift my little finger and the Master would say, 'get in half-a-dozen servants because I'm havin' a party this weekend'."

Wilkins laughed.

"And I knows who that was. That would be the American gentleman you had and he gave big parties, far bigger than my Master ever gave."

"How they drank," Newman went on, "bottle after bottle. I used to wonder how any man could carry so much in him!"

They laughed at this revelation and Sheila thought that they certainly lived in a very different world from the one she had inhabited with her father and mother.

However, she listened to them with great interest realising that now she was out in the world she had to take whatever came her way without being too critical or fussy about it.

When they had finished their luncheon, Newman suggested that they walk to Mrs. Foxton's Agency which was only at the back of Grosvenor Square.

"I was not thinkin' of takin' the horses that short distance," Wilkins said to him. "They'll need a good rest and food the same as we wants and I feel much better now, thanks to your Missus."

"She be a good cook when she has the chance," her husband said proudly. "But the trouble here is that they only entertains once or twice a month and then it's with a team of old people who eats little but talks a lot!"

Wilkins chuckled.

"That might be said about most of us," he muttered.

He scratched his ear before he added,

"Well, we'll be off now and we'll tell you when we comes back what we've discovered."

He looked a little awkwardly at Newman before he said,

"I don't want to ask too much, but will it be all right for us to stay the night if nothin' be fixed up for this lady by then?"

"Of course you can stay here," Newman replied. "No one knows what happens at the top of the house or the bottom and I can give you rooms in both."

Wilkins grinned.

"That's what we wants to hear. So ta-ta for now and we hopes to come back with good news."

When they were outside and were walking towards Grosvenor Square, Wilkins remarked,

"I don't think Newman had the slightest idea who you are and it'd be a mistake for him to find out."

"Why would it be a mistake?" Sheila asked him.

"Because, as you once owned the house, it would be impossible for him not to think it was a feather in his cap that you had come back to ask him for help and to stay in the house without the new owner being aware of who you are."

"You mean he would talk?" Sheila quizzed him.

"Of course he would talk. I used to boast up and down Park Lane that my boss were the oldest Earl in all of England and his wife were acclaimed as the greatest beauty in the Social world!"

Sheila smiled.

"Were they impressed, Wilkins?"

"Of course they were impressed. So I don't want anyone to know that you, the daughter of a great man, is havin' to beg for the bread she eats from those who can afford to employ her."

He spoke scornfully and again Sheila smiled as it all sounded so strange.

Equally she knew that he was speaking the truth.

It would be a great mistake for any of her father's and mother's friends to know that she had been turned out of her home and was being forced to work to keep herself alive.

She gave a deep sigh.

Then, as they reached a house which was obviously the Agency and she could see the name 'FOXTON' blazed over the door, she said quietly,

"What shall I call myself? If no one must know who I am, we must think of a name."

"I be thinkin' you'll want somethin' that be easy to remember, my Lady, otherwise you'll be forgettin' who you are yourself."

Sheila did not smile, because she was thinking that she should have thought of this before.

It was very careless of her not to have realised that, if she was nothing more than a superior servant, she could hardly use her real name, as people would question her as to why she was not in her own home.

They would want to know why the new Earl was not looking after her as he should do.

It was all far too uncomfortable and embarrassing to bear.

She now turned and said to Wilkins in an urgent whisper,

"Please, please think of something quickly."

"I thinks that no one would connect you with your father if you call yourself 'Ash'," Wilkins said. "After all it be an ordinary name, similar to your real one, and it's one you're not likely to forget."

"Of course not," Sheila agreed. "It's a very good idea. I will just be 'Miss Ash' and, if they ask me for a Christian name, which I think unlikely, I will call myself 'Alma' which seems to go well with Sheila."

"Very well, 'Miss Alma Ash' it shall be," Wilkins replied. "By the way I has your references with me."

Sheila looked at him questioningly.

Then he said,

"You must know that Mrs. Foxton and anyone else will want to know who you've been workin' for and why you're leavin'."

"I never thought of that either," she replied, feeling rather inadequate.

"Well, fortunately I thinks of it," Wilkins answered. "I found some references in the secretary's room that have been there for years. I thinks you'll find they'll impress Mrs. Foxton and anyone else who needs a secretary."

Sheila drew in a deep breath.

"Oh, Wilkins, you are so clever. It was so stupid of me not to think of it, but I have never had anything like this happening to me before."

"Then let's hope that you'll not have anythin' like it happenin' again," Wilkins said.

He was feeling in his inside pocket as he spoke.

Then he drew out two envelopes and Sheila could see that they were addressed to her father.

She thought that Wilkins must have taken them out of the secretary's desk because they were obviously several years old.

Wilkins opened one and pulled out the letter that was inside.

She realised that they were the references of the man who had looked after their affairs until unfortunately her father could not afford to pay him any longer.

The man's name was Stephen Aird.

The reference said how brilliant he was and that he was only leaving because he wanted to work abroad and had the opportunity to go to India with Lord Norcomb.

The other reference was an older one saying that Stephen Aird had worked for a famous Peer in the House of Lords and he had left him because he wanted to go to the country.

It was easy for Wilkins to substitute his name with the name of 'Alma Ash' and to change the words 'he' to 'she' by adding an 's'.

"Thank you for being so sensible," Sheila said. "I had totally forgotten that I had to have references. I would have looked very silly if Mrs. Foxton had asked me for one."

"Well, you has two now and, as they're both sayin' you're an angel from Heaven, it would be a strong man or woman who would dare to criticise you!"

Sheila laughed again and slipped the two envelopes into her handbag before they walked in through the door with Foxton's name on it.

Inside there was a staircase going up to the first floor.

When they reached the top, there was a door half-open and Wilkins pushed it so that they could walk through it.

Sheila saw that, sitting against the wall, there were a number of young men and two women.

It was obvious from their appearance that they were servants and she wondered if she should join them.

But Wilkins walked smartly to the end of the room.

An elderly woman was sitting at a desk writing in a large book in front of her.

Although the woman was well aware that they were there, she continued writing for some seconds.

Eventually she raised her head and asked,

"What do you want?"

"This young lady," Wilkins piped up, "requires a position as a secretary, having been an excellent one to the late Earl of Rosswood."

"Oh, he's dead, is he!" Mrs. Foxton exclaimed. "I wondered why I hadn't heard from him or his wife. But I was told they had sold their house in Park Lane and moved to the country."

"That was true," Wilkins replied. "Miss Ash was a really excellent secretary. In fact his Lordship could only speak most highly of her. I've driven her up to London to see if you can find her a new position."

"A secretary," Mrs. Foxton then repeated looking at Sheila with what she thought were rather critical eyes.

"I have two references with me," Sheila said. "I could have brought more, but I rather stupidly left them behind."

She waited for a moment, but, as Mrs. Foxton did not speak, she went on,

"But these two were acceptable to his Lordship and, as I was with him until he died, I know he would not have wanted me to leave him."

She held out the references to Mrs. Foxton.

As she did so, she realised that the envelopes were old and the references had been written five years earlier, but she did not say anything more.

But watching her, Sheila felt almost as if she could read her thoughts.

Mrs. Foxton read both letters, put them back into the envelopes and handed them to Sheila.

"They seem quite satisfactory," she said, "but the difficulty is most people today like a man to work for them and I have two clients waiting for me to find them one."

"As Miss Ash was most successful with both his Lordship and her Ladyship," Wilkins intervened, "it should be no difficulty. As you can understand, she wants to be suited as soon as possible."

"So does everyone else," Mrs. Foxton said almost tartly. "But I can't make places for them and I have to wait until employers come to me for help."

"I know how successful you are," Wilkins replied. "I was only sayin' to someone last week that there was no other Agency in the whole of the City of London as good as yours."

Mrs. Foxton smiled at him and it made her look much more pleasant than she had before.

"Well, I do my best and, if people let me down, I blame myself as well as them for not being up to scratch."

"Well, you'll find Miss Ash has been a real joy to everyone who's employed her," Wilkins insisted.

Mrs. Foxton turned over some of the pages of the large book in front of her and commented,

"The difficulty is – ah, here is one I'd forgotten!"

She bent forward over her book to read what was written.

Impatiently Wilkins asked,

"Be it someone who be well known?"

"Most of my clients are well known," Mrs. Foxton replied stiffly as if he had been insulting to her. "But this one is a very particular person and I'd be very upset if this young lady disappointed him."

"I'm sure she'd never do that," Wilkins retorted. "Who be the person you consider so important?"

As he seemed to be pressing Mrs. Foxton, Sheila was almost afraid that she might be offended.

Instead she answered Wilkins in an awesome tone,

"The Duke of Craigstone."

For a moment Wilkins was surprised.

"The Duke of Craigstone!" he exclaimed loudly. "I thought he was dead."

"No, but he's been ill for over five years to my knowledge," Mrs. Foxton replied. "But he's still alive and the last secretary I sent him left because he said the house was so depressing and he had a chance of going abroad."

"Well, you can't blame him for that!" Wilkins said. "But I thinks, seein' how good she were with her Ladyship and his Lordship, Miss Ash would then be just the right person."

"Well, she can but try," Mrs. Foxton agreed. "It's his Lordship's son, the Viscount Stone, who's asked me to find a secretary."

"We can go there at once," Wilkins offered. "I has to get back to the country, but I do want to see Miss Ash settled before I goes."

"If you're in such a hurry," Mrs. Foxton replied, "you can go to the Duke's house in Grosvenor Square and take Miss Ash there and she must declare that she's come from me."

"She'll do that," Wilkins promised, "and we'll go at once."

"Well, don't be disappointed if Miss Ash is not a suitable person for His Grace," Mrs. Foxton said. "Here's the address and my card to show His Grace that I've seen her."

She scribbled the name 'Miss Ash' on the card and then handed it to Wilkins.

"You've been very kind," he said, "and, if I comes back to tell you they wants a man and not a woman, I'll feel really disappointed."

"I think I've made it clear to His Grace already that a man is not keen on such a gloomy appointment. But, as you're in such a hurry, you might as well go to the Duke and if he says 'no', then just come back here and we'll try again."

She paused before she added,

"People always be coming in and out of this office and there's certain to be a request for a woman secretary."

Wilkins put out his hand.

"Thank you, Mrs. Foxton," he said, "and I feel sure that Miss Ash will not disappoint you."

"I hope not," Mrs. Foxton replied, "but then I can't direct those who are choosing a secretary for His Grace."

"No, of course not," Sheila said, "and thank you so very much for giving me the opportunity."

She shook hands and was aware that, because she had spoken so politely, Mrs. Foxton was looking at her approvingly.

As they walked across the room towards the door, Sheila wanted to give a skip of joy at having a chance of what she felt certain would be a job that even her father would have approved of.

However, she waited until they were outside before she said to Wilkins,

"We have been very lucky."

"We'll have to wait and see," Wilkins replied. "It doesn't sound to me as if the Duke, dyin' or not, be very agreeable. Otherwise there would be people tumblin' over themselves to work for him just because he be a Duke."

"I can easily understand that, Wilkins, but at least he might give me a chance to stay in London and look for something else to do, although I am not at all certain what that could be."

"So you should be grateful to be in a house that be respectable and somewhere your father and mother would have approved of and a roof over your head. If the Duke be dyin', then he can't be a trouble to you in other ways which a girl as pretty as yourself has to cope with."

Sheila stopped still on the pavement.

"I had never thought of that," she said. "Perhaps it would be better if I worked for a lady rather than a man."

Wilkins smiled.

"If the Duke be dyin', he can't do you any harm. All you has to do is to keep the household in order and that's somethin' you managed to do so very well at home, although there ain't been much of a household of late to cause any disorder with!"

Sheila laughed as he meant her to do.

"I expect that the Duke has a large house," she said. "Where does he live?"

"As it so happens on the other side of Grosvenor Square," Wilkins replied. "So we haven't far to walk."

They crossed the square.

After passing several houses, they stopped at a very impressive-looking one in the middle of the square.

It was, Sheila felt, exactly the sort of background the Duke should have.

Wilkins rang the bell.

The door was opened by a footman wearing a very smart uniform.

"We are here from Mrs. Foxton's Agency," Wilkins said, "about the position of secretary."

"Oh, that," the footman said, "I'll tell Mr. Bates you're here."

He hurried away leaving them standing in the hall.

A few minutes later he returned with a man who was quite obviously the butler.

Wilkins realised at once and held out his hand.

"I've come here with this lady from Mrs. Foxton's Agency," he said, "and I am butler to the late Earl of Rosswood. I've brought this lady to London who's been secretary to the late Earl for over six years."

Bates shook hands with Wilkins and replied,

"Viscount Stone, who's the Duke's eldest son, has just left for the country. But he asked me if anyone should be sent for the position to decide in his absence if they be suitable or not."

"Well, I certainly think that you'll find Miss Ash suitable," Wilkins answered. "She has references that we would all be grateful to have in our pockets."

He smiled at Sheila as he spoke and she drew the two letters from her handbag and then handed them to the Duke's butler.

He read them both carefully before he said,

"They certainly seem satisfactory. Perhaps I should now show you the office where the secretary to His Grace works."

He did not wait for them to reply, but went down a corridor which obviously led to the kitchen and the rooms at the back of the house.

When he opened a door, it was to show Sheila an office.

It was exactly what she expected one to be like and it was not very different from the secretary's office at her home.

There was a desk, a safe and a number of tin boxes which she knew contained account books and ledgers.

If they were anything like the ones at home, they were seldom opened from one year to another.

"It seems a very comfortable office," Wilkins was saying. "I thinks as how Miss Ash'd find it easy to work here."

"Yes, of course I would," Sheila agreed.

At the same time she was wondering if there was a great deal to cope with.

If there were a large number of servants in the house, who, if the Duke was ill, would want more from her than she would be able to give them.

As if he knew what she was thinking, Wilkins said,

"You've been such a success everywhere you've been, you can't be anything else here. It's as comfortable as I expected it to be."

"I thought you'd say that," Bates remarked. "To tell the truth we're all very proud of this house which was only built five years ago."

"Who is living in it beside the Duke?" Sheila asked, "if that is not an impertinent question."

"It's the sort of thing Miss Ash will have to know," Wilkins added.

Bates smiled.

"Well, there be his Lordship, the Viscount Stone, and his younger brother Rupert. I'd expect you remember that Her Grace died some years ago and His Grace never recovered from the shock."

Sheila looked at him and exclaimed,

"Oh, I remember now they were at their house in the country when there was a fire. I think I am right in saying that Her Grace was killed when she was trying to save her dog and some puppies it had just given birth to."

Bates beamed.

"You remember right, Miss Ash. It were in all the newspapers at the time. A terrible tragedy and His Grace was never the same after losing his beloved wife in that awful way."

He dropped his voice before he carried on,

"It affected his heart and they says it's only time before he passes on."

"It's very very sad," Wilkins said. "But I'm sure Miss Ash will be able to cope with it and will make things easier for you all."

"Well, I hopes she does that," Bates replied. "As we ain't been paid for three weeks after the last secretary walks out, we'll all be very glad to have our wages up to date and have things shipshape, as one might say."

Sheila smiled.

"I only hope I will be satisfactory," she said, "and I promise to do my best."

Bates smiled back at her.

"I am sure your best is excellent, Miss Ash, and the sooner you gets to work the better."

"I tell you what I'll do," Wilkins suggested. "I'll go back and collect your luggage while you stay here and start to find your way not only round the house but into the safe, where I expect everyone's wages will be."

He pointed to what was obviously a safe in one corner of the office.

Bates grinned.

"You don't miss much, do you?"

"I hope not," Wilkins laughed. "I've been in work of this sort for years and, if I don't know my way around by this time, I'd be ashamed."

"I can say the same," Bates agreed.

Then they were both laughing.

Sheila went over to the desk and put her two letters, which were in her handbag, down on it.

"Here are my references," she said, "and, of course, you might want to show them to His Grace's sons if they question my appointment."

"They'll not question it," Bates replied. "They're only frightened that they might have to do all the work themselves!"

He hesitated before he added,

"They kept telling me that I had to get on and find someone."

"I will do my best," Sheila promised, "but you will have to help me as much as you can and tell me the routine so that I don't make any mistakes."

She smiled at him as she spoke.

Watching her, Wilkins thought it would be a very hard man who would refuse to help anyone so pretty and so polite.

"I'll go and fetch your luggage," he said to Sheila. "Then I'll be getting' back to the country. I'll get into real trouble with his Lordship if I'm not there when he needs me and my wife wants me to be back as soon as I possibly can."

"You have been so wonderful," Sheila said, "and thank you, thank you for all you have done for me."

"Well, if anythin' goes wrong," Wilkins answered in a low voice as if he did not want Bates to hear, "you come straight back to me and the Missus."

"Thank you again," Sheila whispered.

By this time Bates was standing waiting at the door and Wilkins pressed Sheila's hand before he joined him.

After they had left and the door had closed behind them, she took a deep breath.

She could only hope and pray that looking after the Duke's affairs would not be more difficult than her father's estate at home.

She had done everything successfully ever since he had died and then, when her mother was so ill, she had had to see to everything in the house with very few servants.

However, she was quite sure that there would be no lack of help in this house.

But she had to remember everything a secretary did especially when it came to paying the staff their wages and seeing that everything was paid for, also that there was no stealing as happened in so many houses.

'I expect I can do it,' she said to herself. 'In fact I *must* do it. I am very lucky to find somewhere to stay and, if the worst comes to the worst, I will go home and creep into the cellar or the attic where Cousin Thomas will not be able to find me.'

All the same she knew it would be frightening to be in the house when he had turned her out.

Here in the Duke's house, at least for the moment, she was her own Mistress.

If she pleased them, she would be safe and at least she would have somewhere to sleep and eat.

'I am lucky, very lucky,' she told herself again.

Equally because it was all rather intimidating, she sent up a little prayer.

She prayed fervently to God that she would not fail.

And that she would be able to stay here safely and not continue to be afraid.

CHAPTER FOUR

Sheila worked all through day in the office finding out where everything was kept and learning how to open the safe, which was rather antiquated and not as easy as the modern ones.

She gathered from Bates that there was actually a considerable amount of money in the safe.

Therefore she thought that she should count it out to see whether she needed to draw any more from the bank before the wages were paid on Saturday.

There had been no sign the previous evening, after she had arrived, of the relations of the Duke.

She thought when she did meet them the more she understood about their affairs that she was dealing with the more impressed they would be by her.

She had the uncomfortable feeling that they would be disappointed that she was not a man.

So she was therefore rather nervously awaiting her first encounter with them.

And she learnt from Bates that the elder son was staying in the house while he was in London and that the younger son was abroad.

She was glad and relieved to find that the Duke had no daughters.

She felt because she was young and, as most people thought very pretty, female relations would undoubtedly say that she was not capable to do the job and it was better left in the hands of a man.

She had in fact made things fairly shipshape.

She had re-arranged the office to look much more comfortable than it had been when she first entered it.

She tidied away a great number of black tin boxes that were more depressing than anything else and she had asked if she could have some flowers on her writing desk and also on the table by the window.

Bates smiled at her request.

"We ain't used to flowers in the office," he said. "The secretary who's been here in the past had no use for them. But I think flowers cheer up a room and I'll tell the gardener to send some in."

"That is very kind of you," she answered. "Having been in the country, I always miss flowers when they are not there."

She thought as she spoke that she also missed the horses.

She had learnt that the Viscount had some very fine stallions in the Mews stables and was determined when she had time to go and see them.

It was only a case of crossing the garden at the back of the house and the Mews ran parallel with Park Lane.

She was sitting at the desk checking a list of the wages she would have to pay at the end of the week when the door opened and a young man came in.

For a moment she only stared at him wondering who he could be.

Then she thought that he must be Viscount Stone.

"Good morning, Miss Ash," he began. "I have just been told that you have taken up the position of secretary and I can only be grateful to Mrs. Foxton for finding us someone so quickly."

As he drew nearer to the desk, he then looked at her more closely.

She knew instinctively that he was astonished that she was so young.

"I am so delighted to find a place where the work is similar to what I have been doing in the country, my Lord," Sheila replied to him.

"But you cannot have done it for many years," the Viscount answered, "seeing how young you are."

"I think I look younger than I am, my Lord," Sheila said. "Here are the references I obtained before I took up my last appointment. I am afraid that there is not one up to date, as the gentleman I was working for died."

She spoke rather quickly.

She was aware that the Viscount's eyes were still looking surprised as if he thought that she would be very different.

He was extremely handsome and very tall.

She guessed that he was about twenty-five and, as she expected him to be older, she thought that she had been rather stupid in not making any enquiries about him from Bates.

"Now what I came to see you about," the Viscount said, "is that I require a considerable amount of money and Bates informs me that you have it here in the safe, which will save me from going to the bank."

"I have been counting the money this morning, my Lord," Sheila said. "I was surprised, in fact, that so much is kept here in the house. But I understand from Bates that the money for the staff wages is collected monthly from the bank instead of weekly."

The Viscount raised his eyebrows.

"I suppose that saved old Martin a journey to the bank," he remarked rather sneeringly.

"I know how to open the safe," Sheila told him, "although it is rather difficult as it is old. But if you tell me how much you want, my Lord, I will bring it out for you."

"I doubt that there will be enough," the Viscount replied. "Actually I am in rather a difficult position."

He sat down in a chair that was on the other side of the writing desk to where Sheila was sitting.

Because there was a poignant silence and he looked so worried, she asked after a moment,

"Can I help in any way, my Lord?"

"I doubt it," he answered. "As it is a very delicate problem, I don't want to make a fool of myself."

Sheila wondered what it could possibly be that was worrying him.

As he did not continue speaking, she said after a moment,

"I am quite used to solving problems. In fact for the last year or so I have done nothing else. So if I can help you, you will not be asking for anything that I have not heard already."

"I doubt if that is true," the Viscount replied in rather a bitter tone. "In fact this problem is so large that I feel I cannot solve it myself."

"Then please let me help you, my Lord. I really am rather good at solving problems and there is no reason why yours should be any exception."

The Viscount laughed.

"I can easily see why the people you have worked for before found you indispensable. I suppose everyone has difficult problems especially if they have families and mine is even worse than I had expected."

He was speaking in such a serious tone that it made Sheila feel that his problem was a very intractable one.

But she said nothing, thinking it would be a mistake to seem too eager to help.

Perhaps the Viscount was heavily in debt and did not want his father to be aware of it.

There was another silence.

And then after a moment the Viscount said,

"I don't know whether you have yet been told much about the family except that my father is seriously ill and the doctors believe that there is very little chance of him recovering."

"Yes, I was told that," Sheila replied, "and I am so sorry for you, my Lord."

She thought as she spoke how terrible it had been waiting for her father to die and knowing that there was no hope of him surviving, yet feeling that once he had gone she would be completely and absolutely alone.

As if he now realised that she was sympathetic, the Viscount said,

"This particular problem does not concern me, but my younger brother Rupert."

Sheila looked surprised.

"I thought he was abroad," she said. "In fact the butler told me that he had been abroad for some time."

"That is right, Rupert was abroad," the Viscount confirmed. "But he has come back in somewhat unusual circumstances. When I learnt about the situation yesterday, my first thought was to go to the Police."

"The Police!" Sheila exclaimed. "Surely he cannot have done anything wrong, my Lord."

"It is not what he has done," the Viscount replied. "But to put it bluntly he is being held prisoner by some extremely unpleasant Chinese. They require a large sum of money to release him."

Sheila stared at him in astonishment.

"You mean they are blackmailing you, my Lord?" she asked.

"Exactly!" the Viscount answered. "But if I do pay the money they ask, I have a sinking feeling that they may not release him even when they have it and may either kill him or make it impossible for him to say how badly he has been treated."

"It sounds to me horrifying," she whispered slowly. "But how do you know this, my Lord?"

"When I visited my Club yesterday afternoon," the Viscount replied, "I found a letter for me written by my brother and delivered, I suspect on his instructions because he did not wish my father to be upset by the position he now finds himself in."

"Your brother knows then that your father is very ill and not expected to live?" Sheila asked.

The Viscount nodded.

"I sent him a letter to that effect over a month ago to the address he then had in China. I did not expect him to come home, but I said if he wanted to see his father again it was the only thing he could do and he would have to be quick about it."

"So he has come home?" Sheila questioned.

"Yes, he has come home," the Viscount confirmed. "But the people who brought him are determined to benefit in a very large way for bringing him to England. In fact they are asking for ten thousand pounds to be paid to them in English money before they will release my brother."

Sheila stared at him.

"That is a huge sum of money, my Lord. Surely they must be aware that they are not only breaking the law by keeping your brother captive, but if they were found out committing such a horrible crime, they would undoubtedly be arrested and imprisoned."

"In which case my brother will suffer, rather than let him go they would then take him back to China to work there as a slave."

Sheila was silent.

Then she said,

"I see that your problem is very serious, my Lord. At the same time any false step may cost your brother his life."

"That is what I am afraid of," the Viscount replied. "And I commend you for grasping the situation so quickly. Quite frankly I am afraid if I go to the Police, as I ought to do, the Chinese would then disappear immediately, in fact returning to China taking my brother with them."

He gave a deep sigh before he went on,

"If I pay them, it is not only the money that they will take from me, but they may then silence my brother so that he cannot give evidence against them."

"I do think it is a very serious problem for you, my Lord." Sheila said quietly. "But I feel that there must be a way out."

She thought for a moment and then she asked,

"Do these Chinese know who your brother is?"

"I imagine so," he replied, "or they would not ask such a large sum of money for him. His name, as I expect you know is one we all use, that of 'Stone'. He is therefore the Honourable Rupert Stone."

Sheila nodded.

"I feel sure that they must have known who he was, otherwise they would not have asked for as much as ten thousand pounds."

The Viscount nodded.

"Yes, that is obvious and, of course, the one thing I don't want is for there to be any scandal over this or for people to be find out that he is now in such an ignominious position."

He hesitated before he added,

"After all my father, when he was fit and well, was respected and known to be one of the most outstanding Peers, not only in the House of Lords but also at Windsor Castle."

Sheila did not answer at once and finally she said,

"I have an idea, my Lord, but you may think it very strange."

"I would be grateful to hear of any idea that would help get my brother out of this mess," the Viscount replied. "As you can imagine the one thing I don't want, with my father being in such a bad state of health, that it should get into the newspapers, which would distress him more than anything else."

"I can see your point, but my idea is different in a way from what anyone else would suggest to you. But I think if we are clever it will work."

"We?" the Viscount asked her sharply. "How do you come into this?"

"Well, as it happens, my Lord," Sheila said, "I can speak a little Mandarin."

The Viscount stared at her.

"How is that possible?" he asked.

"When my father was alive, he travelled a great deal at one time. One of the places he often visited was China."

She thought, as she spoke, how foolish her father had been where the Chinese were concerned.

He gave them any amount of money they asked him for to invest in their schemes and he was so certain that it would come back a hundred fold.

Of course it did nothing of the sort.

She had helped him write letters either begging for the money to be returned or threatening them if they did not do so.

As it invariably happened, the Chinese themselves disappeared and so it was doubtful if any of their letters reached them.

Sheila had therefore learnt a great deal by writing letters for her father as well as talking to other Chinese he then turned to for help.

She could not help knowing that time after time her father had been taken in by men who were nothing better than crooks.

Inevitably where he was concerned, the money that he believed would come back to him a hundred fold was merely lost for ever.

"Do you really mean," the Viscount was asking her, "that you can talk to these Chinese and tell them that they must release my brother?"

"You have not told me yet, my Lord, who they are or whether you know where he is being held prisoner."

"He is being kept aboard one of their boats which is in harbour, where they are expecting me to take them the ten thousand pounds that they are demanding before setting him free."

"How do you know all this?" Sheila asked.

"He wrote it in the letter left at my Club and told me what was happening to him and begged me to rescue him saying that, if they took him back to China, he will become a slave and be obliged to work without payment and without ever being able to escape."

Sheila drew in her breath.

"This is terrible! Really terrible!" she exclaimed. "How did he get the letter to you, my Lord?"

"He managed to make someone, I don't know who it was, who was bringing food into the Chinese boat, carry this letter to my Club by giving him the last money he had in his pocket and that was very little."

"I think it was very astute of him to find someone to bring you the letter, my Lord. Of course you cannot let your brother be taken to China just to be a slave of these horrible crooks."

"Well, I don't suppose they will cause any trouble if I give them the ten thousand pounds" the Viscount said. "It infuriates me to think that by sheer desperate blackmail they can take so much."

"I have a better idea," Sheila replied. "And I am just thinking it out."

She put her fingers up to her eyes as she spoke.

For a moment she was completely unaware that the Viscount was staring at her as if he could hardly believe what he was seeing.

Sheila took her hands from her eyes.

"I tell you what we must do," she said. "And we need to work quickly, my Lord, because your brother must not suffer any further. Do you know where the ship is?"

"Of course," the Viscount replied.

"Then I suggest that we go there at once," Sheila answered. "But you have to make them believe that you are very important and can help them by your patronage far more than just giving them the amount of money they are demanding."

"I think I understand," the Viscount said.

"What I propose that you should do, my Lord, to get your brother released is to make the crooks believe that we have a better way of helping them than just receiving ten thousand pounds."

"It is a huge amount of money whichever way you look at it," the Viscount murmured.

"Of course it is," Sheila agreed, "and that is why I resent it going to Chinese crooks. We have to play them at their own game and be better at it than they are."

She went towards the safe as she spoke while the Viscount gazed at her.

"We have here all of one thousand pounds" she told him, "which of course they would not think was enough. But my idea is to get your brother released and, if there is any disappearing to do, he can do it with you rather than with the Chinese."

The Viscount stared at her as if he could not believe what he was hearing.

But there was something compelling and positive about her.

It made him think that perhaps, even though it was a gamble, she might well be cleverer than he thought any woman could ever be.

Sheila took one thousand pounds out of the safe.

She put it into a large envelope and handed it to the Viscount.

"I would hate to part even with this," she said, "but at least it is better than giving them exactly what they have asked for. Then I am quite certain that they will trick you in some way."

"If they have the ten thousand pounds, then I think they will have tricked me quite enough," he pointed out.

"What is most essential is that you should get your brother back," Sheila replied. "If the worst comes to the worst, you may have to pay some more."

She saw the Viscount's lips tighten, but he did not say anything.

Then she suggested,

"Now perhaps you would order your carriage, my Lord, drawn by your most impressive horses. If you will give me five minutes to change, I will feel I am a suitable companion to your top hat and frock coat."

She did not wait for the Viscount to answer, but slipped out of the room.

He could hear her running along the corridor.

'She is surely the most original secretary we have ever had,' he said to himself. 'At the same time if she can speak Mandarin, as she says she can, perhaps she could in some way persuade them to part with that foolish brother of mine.'

He had always teased Rupert because he wanted to explore the world and he thought that it was as good an education as he would receive at any University.

Rupert had written enthusiastic letters from India where he had stayed with the Governor General who was a friend of his father.

He had enjoyed not only the attractive women he had met at Simla but had visited the North-West Frontier.

He had been thrilled by the Forts which the English were protecting the country with against the invasion of the restless tribesmen and the menace of Russian expansion.

Then he had travelled on to China with, as he now found, disastrous results.

Upstairs Sheila put on one of the prettiest dresses her mother had bought her.

And a striking hat trimmed with roses, which was more suitable for a garden party at Buckingham Palace.

She strongly wished that she had her mother's pearl necklace, but at least she had the sparkling diamond ring that Wilkins had saved for her.

Picking up her bag and a pair of kid gloves, she ran down the stairs to find the Viscount waiting for her in the hall.

He looked at her in surprise.

Then he said,

"You are certainly very smart."

"Is the carriage waiting, my Lord?" Sheila asked.

"It is outside," he replied.

Without saying anything more she then walked out of the house ahead of him.

Bates opened the door and a footman helped them into the carriage.

It was certainly very elegant and the horses drawing it were outstanding.

As they then drove off, Bates stared after them in astonishment.

With a touch of laughter in his voice, the Viscount said,

"You are certainly surprising, Miss Ash. I am sure that the Chinese will be amazed by your appearance."

"I hope they will be," she replied, "and by you as well, my Lord. I am only hoping my Mandarin, which is somewhat limited, will make them understand how foolish they are being."

The Viscount did not understand, but he thought it would be inappropriate to ask too many questions at this stage.

He was wondering in his mind how anyone who was a secretary and apparently good at her job could also look more glamorous and certainly richer than the majority of the beautiful women he had associated with in the *Beau Monde.*

As the horses were moving very quickly, Sheila and the Viscount did not speak to each other as they headed towards the Embankment.

They drove along it until they were near the Tower of London.

It was then that the Viscount, who had given his instructions beforehand, looked intently out of the window.

He was eager to identify the ship, which the man carrying his brother's note had described to him in as much detail as possible.

Finally he saw it and rapped on the window behind the coachman.

He drove the horses nearer still to the Embankment and pulled them to a standstill.

A footman jumped down to open the door.

The Viscount, having stepped out, held out his hand to Sheila.

As they walked down to the water's edge, she saw that there were boats that people could hire to take them out to a ship anchored further down the river.

Or to one which was too far for them to reach from the Embankment itself.

The Viscount hired the best turned out boat among them, which was not saying very much.

He helped Sheila into it.

They sat side by side and the boatman rowed them slowly towards the rather unimpressive ship that was lying at anchor a little further down the river.

On the Viscount's instructions, when they reached it, the boatman hailed the men on deck that he had brought them visitors.

It was somewhat difficult to climb up the ladder that was let down for them.

But Sheila had done it all before and she stepped aboard without in any way spoiling her fashionable dress or hat.

When the Viscount joined her, she said in Mandarin to the men who were staring at her in considerable surprise,

"We want to speak to your Captain."

Hurriedly they led the way inside what was a rather scruffy ship that badly needed painting.

However, she was well aware that it could carry quite a considerable amount of cargo below decks.

They were ushered into what might be called the Saloon on more civilised vessels.

There was a small table where the Captain of the ship obviously ate and, although the tablecloth was dirty, the chairs were more or less comfortable.

Sheila and the Viscount sat down and waited.

When the Captain did appear, he was, as Sheila had expected, of a very low caste.

At the same time she knew with one look at him that he was extremely crude and sharp-witted when it came to money or the sale of whatever cargo he had brought to London.

He bowed to them politely.

Then Sheila started speaking to him in Mandarin,

"We have come to meet you because we understand you have here on board with you the Honourable Rupert Stone. His brother, the Viscount, is here to represent their father who, I expect you will know, is of very great Social standing in London."

She stopped for breath before she went on,

"He is a very distinguished man, respected not only by everyone in England but by Her Majesty the Queen herself."

She realised as she was speaking that there was a look of astonishment in the man's slit eyes.

She saw that he had noticed the flashing diamond ring on her finger after she had taken off her gloves.

As if he had suddenly become aware that his guests were important and different from what he expected, the Captain snapped his fingers.

A sailor, who had been listening to what was being said, then hurried away to fetch the drinks that were always provided by the Chinese when business was to be talked about.

Then, as if the Captain thought it would be polite to speak to the Viscount, he said,

"You very smart, sir, and it privilege to have you on ship."

Before the Viscount could speak, Sheila responded to the Captain in Mandarin,

"We have come here because we have heard that you have on board the brother of the Viscount, who is also the son of the Duke of Craigstone."

She spoke slowly and saw that the Chinaman was listening intently.

There was a note of excitement in his voice as he replied,

"You bring money, yes?"

"We bring money," Sheila answered. "But I think I should tell you that you are being very stupid."

She was speaking in Mandarin again.

The Viscount did not understand, but the Chinaman did.

"What do you say, I am stupid?" he questioned.

"You have here," Sheila began, "as a prisoner, the son of one of the most influential and respected men in England."

"He pay good money for son?" the Chinaman said.

"Is money really important when, if you have his patronage, you have all the English here in London and in China ready to trade with you because he has done so and because he is aristocratic enough to be very close to the Queen?"

The Chinaman stared at her.

"What you suggest?" he asked.

"I would suggest or rather reprove you for being so foolish," Sheila answered. "The money we give you could be doubled or quadrupled if you have the patronage and the honour of being associated with anyone so important as the Duke of Craigstone and his eldest son, the Viscount Stone, who is here."

She realised more or less that the Chinaman was beginning to comprehend what she was saying.

"You do business with England," she went on, "but it is a small business, not big as it should be. But it could be big if you used the Duke's name as a Patron of your Company."

She paused before she went on,

"If you could say in China, 'the Duke of Craigstone is interested in what we do and buys from us what we take him,' do you not suppose that everyone from the Viceroy down would respect you for doing trade with anyone so influential and so admired by his people and, of course, by yours?"

The Chinaman's eyes narrowed.

She realised that he was beginning to follow what she was saying.

"You have a business," she said, "but is it as big as you would like it to be? Do you bring one ship filled with what is saleable in England or do you bring three, four or five ships all bearing goods that you can sell in return for the best English money?"

At last the Chinaman saw the light.

Bending forward he quizzed,

"How much would Lord Duke take if he gave his name to my business?"

"That is something that you must work out with his Solicitor," Sheila replied. "It depends on how important you are in China."

"I very big and very important," the Chinaman said. "I come to England now eleven times and each time I go back empty – you understand?"

"I do understand that you are being rather foolish," Sheila told him. "If you work with the Lord Duke, he will send back with you what the Chinese want to buy from England. An empty journey makes no money."

The Chinaman brought down his clenched fist quite firmly on the table.

"You right!" he exclaimed, "that clever, that good business."

"Very good business," Sheila agreed. "But first you must please the Lord Duke, who is too ill to come with us today, by giving back his son and charging him nothing for the journey."

The Chinaman's eyes narrowed.

"We ask ten thousand pounds to bring young man here," he said.

"But you will take back to China," Sheila replied, "twenty thousand pounds' worth of goods, which they will want and which everyone will find are completely different from anything they have ever been offered before."

Now there was little doubt that the Chinaman was becoming eager.

"Tell me what Lord Duke wants to sell," he then enquired.

Sheila recited to him a long list of products that she thought would particularly interest the Chinese.

She talked rapidly, using her hands as the Chinese do.

She was aware that the Chinaman was delighted at the idea of becoming such a high-powered trader.

And of having someone who was so close to the Queen as his associate.

"What we must do now," she said, "is to bring the two brothers together so that the Viscount can thank you for bringing his brother home in safety."

Sheila saw that he was listening intently and went on,

"Tomorrow you can work out exactly what you will take back with you to China. In fact I think that the next time you come here, you should bring three or four ships at least."

The Chinaman drew in his breath.

"Do you think we sell everything we have brought and will sell more with two ships?" he asked.

"Quite easily, you might even sell much more. All you need is the Lord Duke's name on your writing paper and you will find he is known in every country in the East as well as in the Mediterranean, who I am quite certain will buy your goods with alacrity once they are told that the Lord Duke is associated with them."

For a moment the Chinaman seemed to bounce up and down on his seat in excitement.

Then he clapped his hands.

Sheila realised that he was telling his men to release the prisoner who was locked in one of the cabins.

"I send for Lord Duke's son," he said, "who's been passenger on my ship. You brought money so I can release him?"

"I have brought you a proposal which will make you great money, very great money indeed," Sheila replied. "It would be a mistake now when the Lord Duke's son is smiling at you to appear greedy. Say you will be ready to fill your ship with all the goods that will be brought to you within the next two or three days."

She smiled at him before she continued,

"At the end you can decide how much money you want in advance and what percentage he will give you on the sales you make when you have carried the goods back to China."

The Chinaman seemed to jump up and down in his seat with joy.

Then he said,

"This very big business. English respect great man with big name. Chinese bring England many, many goods they want."

"Of course," Sheila agreed. "You are so wise and you understand that nothing can be better for you or more significant in the future than for you to represent the Lord Duke abroad."

"I understand, but I think Lord Duke's son should pay for passage," the Chinaman replied.

"But of course," Sheila agreed. "So how much will that be?"

She saw the Chinaman hesitate.

Then he said,

"Five thousand pounds."

"Yes, of course," Sheila replied. "It will come to you tomorrow with all the goods you are to sell and if there is too much then perhaps you can hire another ship to go back with you."

"That good idea. Very good idea."

It was then that there came the sound of someone running up the stairs.

A moment later a young man burst in upon them.

He looked thin and rather dirty.

But the excitement at seeing his brother made him almost incoherent as he exclaimed,

"Charles! How wonderful to see you!"

He almost threw himself at the Viscount, who had risen as he entered.

As he then patted his brother on the shoulder, the Viscount said,

"I want you to thank someone who is staying with us and who is responsible for you being released because she speaks Mandarin."

The young man turned to Sheila and held out his hand.

"Thank you, thank you!" he cried.

"Everything is arranged," Sheila told him, "and all we have to do now is to go home. Perhaps it would be polite if you now thanked the Chinaman for bringing you to your family."

Rupert looked surprised, but obediently held out his hand.

"Thank you very much," he said to the Chinaman, "for bringing me back home. I am sure that my brother has told you how grateful my father will be."

"We have told him in no uncertain terms," Sheila answered quickly. "We will tell you all about it as we drive home. But now I think that we should be going as we have a lot to arrange – to be brought here tomorrow."

She said the last five words in Mandarin so that the Chinaman could make no mistake about them.

In broken English he replied,

"We wait ready for what you send and make big, big profit."

Sheila laughed.

"Of course that is exactly what we want and your English is very good, much better than my Mandarin."

"No! No!" he contradicted, "your Mandarin is very good. I understand you well. But now I work with such important person as Lord Duke, I learn more English."

Sheila rose from her chair and held out her hand with a smile.

"Thank you again," she said, "and tomorrow with the goods will also be a list of what can come later when you return."

"I understand and thank you, lady, thank you," the Chinaman answered excitedly.

He was all bows and smiles as they went out on deck.

While they had been talking, Sheila was aware that at least the ship was now closer to the Embankment.

And it was possible to walk from the deck onto the Embankment itself.

She did so holding the Viscount's hand because she was afraid of slipping and falling into the water.

They were followed closely by Rupert.

As they reached the carriage, the Chinaman stood gazing at it with awe because it seemed so impressive.

As they thanked him again, Sheila stepped into the carriage followed by the Viscount and his brother.

The Chinaman waved to them vigorously and they waved back.

As the horses gathered speed and they drove swiftly along the Embankment, Rupert exclaimed,

"You have done it! You have done it! How did you get me out? You are so clever. I cannot believe I am free."

"You are free entirely due to Miss Ash," his brother said. "I am stunned that she has pulled off the cleverest bit of trickery I have ever listened to."

"Are you saying that you did not have to pay for me?" Rupert asked.

"Not a penny," the Viscount told him. "Like you, I hardly believe it is possible."

"Did you understand what I was saying?" Sheila enquired.

"I did and you were utterly brilliant," the Viscount answered. "Rupert is now free and will disappear. When they find that they have been fooled, they will want their revenge. And so the sooner he is out of London and safe in the country the better I will be able to sleep."

He was speaking to Sheila and then he turned to his brother,

"How could you have been such a fool," he asked "as to get mixed up with people like that?"

"I did not mean to," was the reply, "but I took a trip on one of his ships. I suppose I boasted about my father being rich and the land we had and suddenly I found I was a prisoner. They had every intention of taking every penny they could off me."

"Well, thanks to Miss Ash here we have not paid them anything," the Viscount said, "certainly not the ten thousand pounds they asked for you."

"I am free – free!" Rupert shouted out with delight.

His brother put up his hand.

"Only for the moment and this must not happen again. You will leave early in the morning for the country and stay there until I tell you that it is safe for you to come back."

He looked stern as he went on,

"If you appear in London, they might easily catch you and take you away before we would even realise that you are missing."

Rupert looked serious.

"Would they really do that?" he asked.

"Of course they would," his brother replied. "You must be an idiot to think that we could even get away with only a small amount of money. Those sort of crooks are totally unscrupulous. I have heard stories that people have paid for years before they even caught sight of their loved ones. The Chinese have kept them imprisoned and worked as slaves until every penny they asked for was paid out."

Rupert looked even more worried.

"You don't think they would take their revenge on you?" he asked his brother.

"I think it unlikely that they will know where I live apart from kidnapping me and taking me prisoner, as they have taken you, unless, of course, you have talked."

"I swear to you, Charles, I never said a word of where I lived in London and if I talked of the country they did not understand the English countryside."

"Well, that is just where you are going, Rupert" his brother said, "until it is safe enough for you to come back to London. You can thank Miss Ash from the bottom of your heart because I had no idea how to set you free except by paying out the huge sum they had demanded."

"They would more than likely have doubled it by tomorrow," Rupert answered.

"Then what the hell do you think you were doing with such people?" the Viscount asked him again.

"I went on a trip on one of their ships, as I have already told you," Rupert replied. "The next thing I knew I was locked up and I may tell you that I had very little to eat."

"It's all your own fault. If you had just stayed at home and ridden our horses for your excitement none of this would have happened. For goodness sake make sure in the future that England supplies your needs rather than some obscure Eastern land with thieves, like we have just left, to bleed us to death."

"I am sorry, terribly sorry," Rupert said. "I know I was a fool to talk to them in the first place. I suppose I told them about the horses we had and how magnificent our acres always were."

"So they knew we were rich and were determined to get as much as they possibly could from us," his brother replied. "If anyone was an idiot it was you."

"I have to admit that you are right for once," Rupert confessed. "But how is it possible that this pretty lady can speak Mandarin?"

"I have been wondering that myself. We owe her a very big debt for her brilliance in setting you free without paying a penny for you."

"You should thank my father," Sheila said, "who, when he was alive, travelled a great deal. He used to make me write to the people he had stayed with or did business with, so I gradually picked up a great number of words and some of them have been no use to me before today."

"The fact that you know Mandarin was of great use to me," Rupert said, "and thank you, thank you. I think I would like to buy you a present and you must tell me what you would like to have."

Sheila smiled at him.

"I will be grateful for anything you give me. But if money is short, please don't be too extravagant."

"Money short!" Rupert exclaimed looking directly at his brother. "Surely Papa has not run riot with all the family heirlooms."

"No, of course not," his brother answered. "But we just cannot afford to pay thousands of pounds to set you free from every unpleasant prison. So you must remember that, although we are rich, there are always a great number of expenses and quite frankly we need every penny."

Listening, Sheila thought with amusement that they had no idea, either of them, what real poverty was like.

Since her father had lost everything he possessed and had sold all that was saleable, they had been in an even worse position than Rupert had been as a prisoner.

What she minded more than anything else was that people who had worked for them for years had to leave because they could not pay their wages.

The village had shrunk and the older people, more than anyone else, had suffered. She knew that it was no use grumbling and no use in asking people to understand.

But she hoped that never again would she have to turn people out, who had served them faithfully for years and years.

She had realised that, if her father went on losing every penny they possessed, they would soon be in a state of starvation.

'If only I could have saved *us* as I managed to save Rupert,' she thought, 'I would not feel as I feel now utterly alone in a world I no longer belong to.'

CHAPTER FIVE

There was certainly no sign of poverty in the house in Grosvenor Square.

The Viscount's friends came to the house for dinner and on several evenings, when Sheila was going up to bed, she would hear them leaving.

She knew that they were either telling each other amusing stories or teasing some unfortunate man over the trouble he was in, undoubtedly with a woman.

She found that the Viscount was always very polite to her.

In fact he treated her as if she was a lady and not a servant.

It was interesting for her to realise that the servants themselves looked on her as something superior to them.

They were always respectful and addressed her as 'Miss Ash' and never by her Christian name.

"One day,' she thought to herself, 'I must write a book about the differences in human behaviour. How it varies so much from one person to another simply because they were born in a different position rather than the fact that their character has developed over the years.'

She thought that it would be a rather amusing book and then she told herself sharply that she had no time for books.

That was certainly true.

There were always plenty of bills to be paid by the secretary, also a number of letters that had to be written, some questioning the prices charged for repairs and others to tradesmen of one sort or another.

More important than anything else were the private letters that Sheila either accepted or refused for the endless invitations that seemed to pour in for the Viscount.

She had learnt that he had been away from England quite considerably in the past until his father was so ill and so he had now taken over all the duties that his father had performed with the previous secretary.

He dictated his letters to her so quickly that she had difficulty in keeping up with him.

She often had to make up the end of a letter with an idea of what he had said rather than his actual words.

He never seemed to notice it, but signed the letter quite happily.

She therefore congratulated herself on being more efficient than she had anticipated.

Then unexpectedly one evening as she was tidying up her office for the evening the Viscount came in.

"Good evening, Miss Ash," he began. "Have you finished your day's work?"

"It has been a hard day's work," Sheila answered with a smile. "But now I am glad to say I have cleared up everything until tomorrow morning when, of course, I start again."

"Have you anything to do this evening," he asked, "like being taken to a theatre or dining with a young man?"

Sheila stared at him thinking that perhaps he was trying to be funny.

Then she replied,

"If you want to know what I am doing, I am going upstairs to read a book I borrowed from your library, which I am finding exceedingly interesting."

To her surprise the Viscount gave what she thought was a sigh of relief before he enquired,

"I wonder if you would do me a great favour."

"Of course I will if it's possible, my Lord," Sheila replied.

"Then would you come to dinner tonight? I have just discovered that we are thirteen and the ladies present, if not the gentlemen, are very superstitious."

"Thirteen!" Sheila exclaimed. "I am rather scared of that number, in fact very much so simply because we were thirteen at the table the night before my mother was taken ill. Although she did not die, she never completely recovered. So I have always been wary of thirteen ever since."

"Then you will dine with me tonight?" the Viscount insisted.

"I will be delighted to do so if you really want me, my Lord," Sheila answered.

"I definitely want you, as it is a birthday celebration for my guest of honour and so we will all dress up and the ladies will undoubtedly be wearing their most attractive gowns."

Sheila knew that he was hoping against hope that she would have something really smart to wear.

Quietly she said,

"I will try not to make any mistakes, my Lord."

"You will understand," he said, looking somewhat uncomfortable, "that I will introduce you as a friend of mine and not say what position you have in this house."

As he had obviously been embarrassed by what he had to say, Sheila answered him,

"I will be very pleased to be a friend of yours, my Lord, and I promise I will not disgrace you in any way."

"I did not mean that," the Viscount replied quickly.

She knew that he was feeling slightly awkward at asking someone who he employed as a servant to eat in the dining room.

To put him at his ease, Sheila asked,

"What time would you like me to be downstairs? I think that it would be wrong to ask your butler to announce me."

"Yes, yes of course, I had not thought of that," the Viscount agreed. "My guests are asked for a quarter to eight. Therefore, if you could be with me for seven-thirty, there will be no question of Bates announcing you."

"I will be down at seven-thirty," Sheila said quietly and walked towards the door.

"Thank you, I am extremely grateful," the Viscount answered. "I do hope you will enjoy the evening."

"I am sure I will, my Lord."

When she walked up the stairs to her room, she was thinking how few evenings' enjoyment she had had since she had grown up.

When her father and mother had been well enough, there always seemed to be people dropping into the house.

But, as they were in the country, they were mostly local friends, who wanted to only talk about the horses and the various Race Meetings that took place regularly on her father's land.

He himself was nearly always away and, when he had returned and entertained, it was usually someone with whom he was doing business, who Sheila found not only boring but at times unpleasant.

When she had been small, they would chuck her under the chin.

And when she was older they would then pay her fulsome compliments that were always badly worded and seemed rather impertinent and made her feel uneasy.

It would be amusing, she thought, to meet people from what the servants called 'her own class' and see what they were like.

Of course, if she had come out as a *debutante*, as she should have done, she would have been asked, because of her father's title and her mother's beauty, to a great number of parties, starting with those that were patronised by Royalty down to amusing dinner parties at home.

They were joined after dinner by other *debutantes* so that they could dance in the big ballroom at the back of the house, which had been built at the same time as the house itself.

'Now what shall I wear to impress him?' she asked herself.

She was amused by remembering that he had been afraid she would not have a decent evening gown to wear.

She had hung up all her own clothes which were not particularly outstanding in one wardrobe.

In another wardrobe in the dressing room opening out of her bedroom, she had placed all the things belonging to her mother.

There were at least six very lovely evening gowns to choose from, which had not become outdated in any way by fashion as some of the other clothes had been.

Finally she chose one that she had admired herself and had longed to have a suitable occasion to wear it.

It was a very thin, pale blue chiffon ornamented with tiny bunches of pink flowers. Flowers glittering with diamanté diamonds encircled the top of the bodice and the waist.

Her mother had a very small waist and, as Sheila had one too, the dress fitted her perfectly.

The only item that was missing, she mused, was the diamond necklace that her father had sold, although her mother had given it to her as a present.

So round her neck she tied a bow of ribbon which matched the pink flowers.

Her mother's bracelets had also been sold, but the dress had little bracelets of the soft chiffon surmounted by a collection of tiny pink roses that made her fingers appear very long and white.

It made the whole ensemble look exceedingly smart and very up to date.

She remembered that her mother had worn roses in her hair the last time she had worn the dress at a local Hunt Ball.

Fortunately some clever lady's maid had attached them to the dress in case they should get mislaid and it was only a question of undoing the safety pins.

When she had arranged the roses in her hair, Sheila thought without being too conceited that she really looked attractive, so different from the very plainly dressed young secretary who had been sensible enough to arrange her hair neatly in a bun at the back.

She then took one last glance at herself in the long mirror that was attached to the wall.

She could see herself from the top of her head to the soles of her feet.

Then, because she was laughing with joy at looking so smart, she dropped herself a curtsey.

"Tonight," she said to her reflection, "you are Lady Sheila Rosswood again and Miss Ash can stay upstairs!"

Because she was excited at the idea of attending a party, which in her life had been few and far between, her eyes were shining.

She looked, when she entered the drawing room, as expectant as any pretty girl would be if she was attending a party given in her honour.

The Viscount was smartly dressed in his evening clothes and was facing the fireplace.

When he caught sight of Sheila in the mirror, he thought that she must be one of his friends.

He turned round swiftly and gave a gasp when he realised the fairy-like creature entering the room was in fact his secretary, Miss Ash.

He stared at her for a moment.

Then he walked towards her saying,

"Your Fairy Godmother must have waved her wand over you. I can only tell you that you look very beautiful. I am afraid my other female guests will leave immediately feeling that they have been eclipsed!"

Sheila laughed.

"That is more or less what I hoped you would say, my Lord, but not so effusively. As it is, I will merely say, thank you, kind sir."

"I think that you are very efficient and you have proved yourself cleverer than I ever expected when you saved Rupert from those Chinese crooks," the Viscount said. "But tonight you will undoubtedly be the belle of the ball in a very different scenario."

As he finished speaking to her, there was silence for a moment before he said,

"That sounds very rude. I am trying to compliment you, but there are no words to tell you how magnificent you are in every way."

"Now you are making me shy," Sheila replied. "If you say anymore, I will go upstairs and put on a very dull black dress so that no one will notice me."

"I will prevent you from doing anything so cruel and unkind," the Viscount answered. "You are going to make this dinner party a great success and I know every man present will tell me so when they say goodnight."

"We can only wait and see, my Lord."

The Viscount crossed the room to where there was a bottle of champagne in a golden ice-bucket.

"We must drink your health," he said, "because you look so lovely. At the same time I am wondering if you are going to think my party is not grand enough for you."

"Now you are being modest. I am so delighted to be at your party because for personal reasons I have been to very few parties since I grew up."

"I can hardly believe that is true," the Viscount answered, "considering the way you are dressed tonight."

"I will let you into a secret," Sheila confided, "but you must promise not to tell anyone."

"You can trust me."

"This gown is not mine," she began, "it belonged to my mother. She was very beautiful and I remember seeing her going to a Hunt Ball in it and hearing my father saying that she would undoubtedly be 'the belle of the ball'."

As she finished speaking, Sheila suddenly thought that she was very stupid to say all this about her family.

It was because she was enjoying so much the *tête-á-tête* she was having with the Viscount that she had, for the moment, forgotten that, as far as he was concerned, she

95

was just an ordinary secretary, someone to cope with the household expenses and when he required them, official letters.

It was really because since her mother's illness, she had had so little chance of being dressed up or of talking to men who were friends and not employees.

It was then, as the Viscount handed her a glass of champagne, that the door opened and Bates announced in a stentorian voice,

"Lady Swanson, my Lord."

Sheila turned round and saw coming in through the door someone she had read about in the Court columns of the newspapers.

She was aware that she was one of the beauties who always appeared in the ladies' magazines.

She was indeed exceedingly beautiful in an almost provocative way and she was wearing a gown that matched the emeralds around her neck.

The feathers that fluttered at her hips were echoed by the same feathers ornamenting her dark hair.

She was certainly striking.

As the Viscount hurried towards her, she said in a seductive voice,

"You told me to be early, dearest Charles, so that we can have just a few minutes together before your guests arrive."

She gave a spiteful glance at Sheila as she spoke, who wondered if she should withdraw and leave the two of them alone, when to her relief Bates appeared again.

He announced three more guests.

Two were a young married couple and the other a young man, who, after he had shaken hands with his host, moved quickly towards Sheila.

"I don't think we have met before," he said. "May I introduce myself because I am very anxious to know your name?"

Sheila smiled.

"Perhaps it would be more polite for us to wait to be introduced," she replied.

"Nonsense!" he exclaimed. "I am Richard Hilton and, as I am known as an explorer, I am always ready to explore something new and beautiful before anyone else gets there."

As Sheila had moved a little way from the Viscount when Lady Swanson was announced, they were now close to the mantelpiece.

The other guests, who were now arriving one after another, were nearer the door on the other side of the room.

"If you are an explorer, I hope that you will tell me what you have found," Sheila said.

"I have just found *you*," he replied. "As I would like to talk about you, my first question is, why have I not seen you before?"

Sheila laughed.

"I think perhaps the answer to that is because you are either getting lazy or bored. Actually I have not been in London for a very long time."

"Ah!" he retorted. "So that is your excuse. But now I have found you I am not going to be so stupid as to lose you. I only hope that we sit next to each other at dinner."

Because it was all so new and amusing for Sheila, she was enjoying herself.

Although she felt inclined to laugh out loud when everyone she was introduced to said,

"I don't think that we have met before. Are you a newcomer to London life or have you been hiding away somewhere?"

Sheila thought it was easier to say that she had been in the country and also in mourning for the last six months which made it seem excusable why she had not attended any parties.

"If you ask me," one young man said, "you have just dropped from the sky."

He was clearly intrigued at meeting someone who was beautiful enough to draw the attention of almost every man in the room.

In fact, by the time everyone had arrived and they were moving into the dining room, Sheila felt as if she had never enjoyed a party so much.

To her delight and certainly to his, she was sitting next to the explorer, Richard Hilton, at dinner.

It was his place card in front of him that told her he was *Sir* Richard Hilton.

"You are where I wanted you to be," he enthused as they all sat down. "It saves me from making a scene and saying that, as I found you when I least expected to do so, I have every right, as I am explorer, to continue my search. Which means, in simple words – do please tell me about yourself!"

Sheila chuckled.

"That would be very dull. It would be much more interesting if you told me what you had found recently and why you became an explorer."

"I suppose I ought to say because I had hoped to find someone like you," he replied. "But actually it was because it gave me an excuse for travelling to parts of the world where no one went and people were interested in my discoveries because they had not heard about them before."

He was, however, so anxious for Sheila to tell him about herself that it was only at the end of dinner she found out that what he really discovered was unknown crimes in foreign countries that had never been written about.

In many cases his discoveries had not only played a part in the history of the country itself, but also produced strange and unusual weapons.

Up to now these weapons had only been seen in historical museums.

"It must be really thrilling for you when you find something that no one has found before," Sheila said. "It is something I would love to do myself."

"You are certainly worth exploring," Sir Richard said again, "and I will be extremely annoyed if you then disappear when the evening is over back to the Fairyland from which you have undoubtedly come!"

Sheila wondered what he would say if she said that she was only going back to the secretary's office in the other part of the house.

Then she knew that she was most unlikely to see him again.

But it would be amusing to think that perhaps he would be searching for her at other parties or confronting the Viscount with a number of intimate questions that she was certain he would not want to answer.

One thing, however, which she had noticed at the party was that Lady Swanson was making it quite clear that the Viscount belonged to her.

After dinner they moved into the music room.

Not to dance, as they might have done on other occasions, but because one of the Viscount's guests played the piano.

One female guest, another Countess as it happened, sang.

Originally she had been singing professionally, but now, since her marriage, she only sang for charities.

Sheila was thrilled at the Countess's very beautiful voice.

She enjoyed the music played by a professional performer, who she learnt from Sir Richard was one of the most popular men in London.

"Why do you say that about him?" she asked Sir Richard, who was still at her side even after they had left the dining room.

"Because he is so brilliant at the piano," he replied. "At times, when it suits him, he plays at the theatre or at parties for charity."

He paused before he went on,

"But he plays for us because we are his friends, especially our host, the Viscount, who was at school with him."

"Is he paid for his performance?" Sheila enquired.

"Oh, I think he takes whatever they offer him," Sir Richard answered. "But he is a rich man and has given a great deal to charity over the years."

Sheila had so much to absorb and so much to learn about the people present that almost before she was aware of it the clock was now pointing to the early hours of the morning.

At last, rather reluctantly, some of the couples rose to leave.

"We have to remember we need our beauty sleep," one lady said, "considering that there is a party every night and I will be very disappointed, my dear Charles, if I do not see you at the Bridgewater's tomorrow night."

"I will certainly be there," the Viscount promised. "You must spare me two dances at least."

As he spoke obviously lightly, Sheila saw the anger on the face of the Countess who was close to him.

'So she must be very much in love with him,' she thought to herself. 'I wonder if he is in love with her.'

It was difficult to judge as the Viscount was being charming to all his guests and, Sheila thought, flattering them in the same way that he had flattered her.

Finally, as they began to say goodnight, there was only the Countess left.

Sheila was quite certain that she wanted to be alone with the Viscount.

At the same time she was not certain whether the Viscount had said that she was staying in the house and it was therefore difficult for her to leave unless the Countess left first.

Whilst she was thinking about it, the Viscount, who had been seeing someone into the hall, came back into the room to say,

"Your carriage is at the door, Dorina."

"What about this lady?" the Countess then enquired indicating with her hand to Sheila.

"Oh, she is staying for the night," the Viscount had replied before Sheila could speak.

"You did not tell me that," the Countess retorted.

Now there was a sharp note in her voice which told Sheila without words how much it annoyed her.

"I will explain it to you as we go to your carriage," the Viscount suggested tactfully.

He put his arm through hers and drew her towards the door.

As they passed through it, the Countess turned and looked back at her and Sheila thought that if she could have knocked her down she would have done so.

As she disappeared and the room was empty except for herself, Sheila walked to look in the mirror over the mantelpiece.

She mused as she did so that she had never enjoyed an evening more.

She knew now that she had missed something very exciting in not being allowed to 'come out' as a *debutante* when she reached the age of eighteen.

'I have missed all this,' she reflected. 'Perhaps if I had been in London instead of struggling to keep Mama alive and helping Papa in the country, I might have been married by this time with children of my own.'

What she really minded leaving behind more than anything else were her dogs.

They had meant so much to her and she knew that they would miss her as much as she missed them.

She felt sure that Wilkins and his wife would look after them and then perhaps one day she would be able to have them with her.

She was thinking of them rather than herself and still looking in the mirror when the Viscount came back into the room.

"I don't have to tell you," he said, "that you were magnificent this evening."

"I am afraid your friend the Countess was annoyed that I am staying here," Sheila replied. "We should have thought of that before and you could have pretended to show me into a carriage while I hid upstairs."

"I did not think of that," he now admitted. "She is jealous of you because you look so young and so beautiful. Everyone said the same tonight and they wanted to know where I had found you."

He laughed as he added,

"It would have been disillusioning to have said to them, 'in my secretary's room in the back corridor'."

Sheila laughed too.

"The only chance of getting any sort of peace from my other male guests," the Viscount continued, "is to tell them you have gone back to Fairyland where you came from."

"You would be better to make it India or Hong Kong," Sheila said, "then they will soon cease to look for me."

"I am not so sure of that," the Viscount answered. "Therefore tomorrow, when you go out, disguise yourself which, of course, you are a past master at doing."

"I will do my best, my Lord. But, as I leave by the side door, perhaps they will not think of searching for me in the back corridors and will soon give up the chase."

"I am not so sure about that," the Viscount replied. "But thank you a thousand times for helping me out this evening and for being such a success."

"It has been very wonderful for me," Sheila said. "I know now what I have missed."

As she spoke, she thought once again that she was being indiscreet and should have kept silent.

However, the Viscount did not seem to notice as he closed the piano lid.

"I will be giving another party soon," he remarked, "because all my guests have asked for another one. They would be particularly disappointed, I am sure, if you did not appear."

"Then please be careful, my Lord, what you say as to where I have gone," Sheila replied. "Otherwise they may suspect I have wings!"

"I think they presume that already. In fact by the end of the evening I was beginning to think that you were not real but had come down like manna from Heaven the moment I needed you."

"I hope that is what you will continue to think," Sheila said, "and now goodnight and thank you, thank you for a really wonderful evening. I enjoyed every minute of it."

She did not wait for the Viscount to answer her, but slipped out of the door and ran down the passage towards the stairs.

Sheila was not aware that, after she had gone, the Viscount stood for at least ten minutes gazing at the door she had just disappeared through.

There was a strange expression on his face.

*

The next morning Sheila was back in her office at nine o'clock promptly.

Since she had arrived, she had thought it essential for her to have some good fresh air as it was a delight that she missed after always living in the country.

She therefore went into the garden in the centre of the square and walked round it several times.

The next day she was brave enough to go into Hyde Park by herself.

Walking among the trees she thought for a moment that she was at home with the dogs at her feet with nothing to worry her except that her father was losing more money as usual and he would come home eventually with empty hands.

'Surely he had to win just once or perhaps twice,' she had told herself when she said her prayers every night.

But it seemed as if even God and His angels could not help her with this request.

This morning, after she came back to her office, she felt for a few moments as if it was imprisoning her and she longed to be free.

Then, as she heard the Viscount coming down the corridor, she thought that she must be very careful not to impose on the fact that last night she had spoken to him as if he was an equal.

He was holding two letters in his hand as he walked up to her desk.

"Good morning, Miss Ash," he said.

"Good morning, my Lord," Sheila answered rather accentuating the word 'Lord'.

She wanted to show him that she had not changed in any way simply because he had been kind enough to ask her to his private party.

The Viscount sat down in the chair on the other side of her desk.

"I want to thank you again for helping me last night and I am wondering how we can repeat that excellent party which everyone enjoyed so much."

"Perhaps the next time you will not be thirteen."

"I will make sure I am," the Viscount replied. "It is no use pretending that you were not a success at the party, as you undoubtedly were. I am wondering how many other ways you have of surprising me."

"I noticed that the Honourable Rupert was not there last night," Sheila said, changing the subject. "Did you not ask him?"

"Of course I asked him," the Viscount answered, "but he was very anxious to visit a friend he had been with at University. He had made every effort to prevent him from getting mixed up with those dreadful Chinamen."

He paused before he went on,

"As his friend was going back to Oxford today, it was his only chance to tell him all that had happened to him, now it is safe for him to come back to London after being hidden in the country for so long"

"I think that he should write the whole saga down in a book," Sheila suggested.

"That is where you will find yourself if Sir Richard has his way," the Viscount answered.

Sheila laughed.

"He was so very certain that he was an unbeatable explorer and he kept telling me that no one could deceive him by being what they are not."

"But you *did* deceive him," the Viscount pointed out.

"I hope so, my Lord," Sheila answered.

"I am certain you did," the Viscount added. "He told me when he left that he had every intention of seeing you again and would we both have luncheon with him tomorrow at *The Grand Hotel*."

Sheila was silent for a moment.

Then she asked,

"How did you answer him, my Lord?"

"I told him that we would be delighted to do so," was the reply.

Again there was silence.

Then Sheila quizzed him,

"Are you going to tell him that I am employed as your secretary?"

"Only if you think it wise for me to do so. Quite frankly I don't want him to snatch you from me. Not at the moment when things are so difficult. It is only a question of time before my poor father leaves us."

Sheila thought it rather odd that the Viscount had given a party in the house when his father was so ill.

But, as there was no possible way that the Duke could have been disturbed by it, it was obviously far more comfortable for his son to entertain his friends at his home than if he went out to a restaurant or a hotel.

She could only think that the Viscount was more sensible than she would have been in the same position.

"What I am really saying to you," he said, "is, are you prepared to come with me to *The Grand Hotel* the day after tomorrow? If you don't want to be worried day after day, I think it would be wise to keep him thinking that you are just a friend and not connected with me in any other way at all."

"I will do whatever you think best," Sheila replied. "It might well be embarrassing if he knew that I was only a secretary and not the glamorous creature he thought me to be."

"I think 'just a secretary' hardly describes you," the Viscount answered, "considering what you have done for me by rescuing Rupert from the Chinese, also helping me in the most amazing manner over being thirteen at dinner. I am sure that Hilton is right in thinking that you are someone very special who he is reluctant to lose contact with."

Sheila laughed.

"You make it all sound wonderful and I can only thank you once again for being so kind, my Lord."

"I am still deeply in your debt. So I am thinking of how I can thank you by giving you something you really want."

"Oh, you don't have to do that," Sheila told him. "It would be very silly if one could not help someone in danger without being rewarded for it."

"But I do insist on rewarding you. I want to know what you would like. A fur coat? Diamonds? And what woman has ever refused those?"

"I don't think that they are at all suitable for me in the position I am in now," Sheila replied.

"So it is not a position you have held in the past," he enquired, "although you seem to be very efficient at it?"

"Now you are being like Sir Richard," she chided. "You are trying to make me into a mystery and that is what I wish to remain."

"So you admit you are a mystery and that you are not who you pretend to be!"

There was a pause before Sheila asked him,

"Do I have to answer those questions?"

"Are you refusing to do so?" the Viscount asked.

"For a moment, yes. If I am a mystery, then it is a good thing for me to be one, considering where I am and who you are, my Lord."

"If you tried to invent anything more intriguing, you would certainly fail," the Viscount said. "I lay awake all last night thinking about you and I will do the same tonight."

Sheila was musing how angry that would make the Countess if she was aware of it.

So she therefore said nothing.

After a while the Viscount rose from his chair and said,

"If you will not tell me what I can give you, I will buy something which I think will suit you and, if you are disappointed, it will be your fault and not mine!"

He walked towards the door.

Then he turned back to say,

"Don't forget about our luncheon appointment at *The Grand Hotel* tomorrow. You cannot make Sir Richard Hilton worry about you as well as me!"

He was gone before she could think of an answer.

Then she laughed.

She certainly had enjoyed herself last night.

It was wonderful and really exciting to think that tomorrow at one o'clock she would be having luncheon at *The Grand Hotel*, not only with Sir Richard Hilton but also with the Viscount.

CHAPTER SIX

Although she was tired when she climbed into bed, Sheila found herself worrying over what she should wear tomorrow.

She thought it would be a big mistake for her to be overdressed as she had been tonight.

She must step back into being the quiet unimportant secretary rather than the glamorous young woman she had appeared this evening.

She was quite certain that the Countess was being as catty as she could be about her, while the other women present were jealous, because she had received a great deal of attention from the gentlemen.

'It was stupid of me,' she thought. 'I should have dressed very plainly looking like the Vicar's daughter and then no one would have noticed me.'

At the same time she could not help being thrilled at receiving a great number of compliments, some of them from the Viscount.

'There is no doubt,' she thought, 'that the Countess will scratch my eyes out if she ever sees me again. So then the sooner I go back to my rightful place in the secretary's office the better.'

Yet she could not help being excited by it all.

She kept thinking that, if her father had been alive and one of his 'get rich quick' schemes had come off, she would have been able to take her place amongst the elite who filled the Social columns of every newspaper.

Finally she fell fast asleep only to wake up in the morning feeling animated because she was going out.

She knew that *The Grand Hotel* was one of the hotels in London where Society people met especially for luncheon because it overlooked the River Thames.

She had read about the hotel in quite a number of magazines.

When she was half-dressed, she went over to the wardrobe in her room to see which of the dresses she had unpacked she should wear.

Some were still in the boxes, as she had been quite certain that she would not want them.

They were far too grand for a mere secretary!

Because both she and her mother had been so fond of colour, when she opened the wardrobe door, the colours seemed almost to jump out at her, pink, blue, green, yellow – all the colours of the rainbow.

So she decided that there was nothing there that she was looking for.

It was indeed difficult to find a dress that was not, she thought, either too bright in colour or else too smart.

Although her mother had been dead for some years, her clothes were still fashionable simply because they had been so beautifully made.

There was no question of them looking shabby or for that matter out of date.

Finally she chose a plain fairly dark blue dress with a pleated skirt.

With it was a bolero-style jacket that was trimmed with satin ribbon, which was the same colour but paler and it made the whole outfit look very distinctive.

'If I am too smart, then I am too smart,' she thought to herself.

She said the same words when she found the hat that went with it. This was of blue straw and matched the dress.

It was trimmed with small blue feathers which were the colour of the satin on the jacket.

As she looked at herself in the mirror, she thought it would be impossible for anyone to guess that she was just a secretary.

But in the circumstances there was really nothing she could do about it.

Unfortunately she had no jewellery to wear.

She knew that, if her mother's pearl earrings had not been sold by her father, she would have wanted to wear them under the brim of her hat.

'I am really asking too much,' she thought. 'I am so lucky in my position to be asked out to luncheon at *The Grand Hotel*. It is ridiculous to wish for more. If it was not for Wilkins, I should now be hiding in the coalhole or walking round the village hoping that someone would be kind to me.'

The scenario was so horrible that it was best not to think about it.

Instead she searched for a pair of clean gloves and the handbag that had been her mother's.

Eventually she realised that it had taken her nearly two hours to dress.

When she went down to the office feeling very self-conscious, she fortunately did not see any of the servants, who would have thought it strange that she was so dressed up.

Even stranger as it was still early in the morning.

She had dressed ready to go out because she knew that it would be a mistake to keep the Viscount waiting.

She was not exactly sure when he would fetch her from her office.

There were as usual a number of letters already on the desk waiting for her and quite a number of them were bills.

These she put ready to write out the cheques to go with them when she had time.

The letters were mostly invitations for the Viscount and these she placed on one side for him to see whether he wished to accept or refuse the parties and other occasions that he was formally invited to.

She had just finished opening the letters when the Viscount came into the office.

"Good morning," he said. "I see you are ready as I hoped you would be. As it is such a lovely day, I thought we might drive into Hyde Park and along the Embankment before we settle down for luncheon."

"That is a lovely idea, my Lord," Sheila replied. "I have a number of invitations for you, which you might like to see before we leave."

"They can wait," the Viscount answered her. "The horses should be at the door by this time and the sooner we get away the less likely we are to be stopped by people asking us to do a number of things we don't want to do."

Sheila laughed.

"That happens to us all," she said.

"It certainly happens to me. I am going to go very carefully through the invitations, because before you came I spent one or two extremely boring evenings because I did not know what to expect before I arrived."

"I see that you must be very careful who you accept and who you refuse," Sheila said.

"Well, come along then," the Viscount urged, "and let me say you look so smart that all the eyes at *The Grand Hotel* will be on you and not me."

"You need not worry about that," Sheila answered. "You are always in the newspapers wherever you go and that is a compliment in itself."

"I am not certain it is," he replied. "Later I will tell you why."

Sheila wondered what he meant by that.

But, as he was talking, he was leading the way out of the office and down the corridor towards the hall.

Bates had the door open and outside Sheila could see that they were travelling in a very smart chaise drawn by two extremely well bred horses.

She wanted to pat them and to talk to them as her father had always taught her to do.

But a footman was holding the door of the chaise open for her and the Viscount went round to the other side to climb into the driving seat.

There was a groom in a very smart livery behind them and, as they drove off, Bates and the footman bowed, and then the horses moved into Park Lane.

The Viscount had been right in saying that it was a lovely day. The sun was shining brightly and the trees in Hyde Park seemed almost to glow.

They drove around and, when they reached Rotten Row, there were quite a number of people who waved to the Viscount.

Some women, Sheila thought, looked at her a bit critically, as if they wondered who she was and why she was a newcomer as far as they were concerned.

Finally after passing Buckingham Palace they came to the Embankment.

Driving with a skill that Sheila really appreciated, the Viscount slowed the horses down so that she could see the Thames and the boats moving along it.

"Are you enjoying yourself?" the Viscount asked.

"You know I am," Sheila replied. "I think that the Thames is always beautiful with the sun shining. I would like to be in one of those ships that are going off into the unknown perhaps to explore parts of the world they have never seen before."

"It is what I enjoy doing myself and I have been promising myself ever since I returned home that I would creep away from all the London Social entertainment and find an intriguing country I have never visited, which will be an excitement from the first moment I set foot on it."

"That is just how one should feel when one is going somewhere new, my Lord. If one is disappointed later, one has still enjoyed the first thrilling moments because it will be so different from what one has found before."

"You are so right," the Viscount agreed. "I hope one day that you will explore more of the world than you have already done."

Because Sheila knew that this was most unlikely, she said nothing.

She merely bent forward to look between the trees at the river.

They drove as far as the Tower of London and then went a little further still.

It was half-past twelve when the Viscount turned back and drove very slowly towards the Strand and then he headed for Trafalgar Square.

Sheila knew that *The Grand Hotel* had very good music played by distinguished performers when the hotel guests were eating either their luncheon or dinner.

She had often thought that it was a place she would like to visit.

When they walked in and found that Sir Richard was waiting for them, she thought this would be something to remember when she was back in her office and when her meals were brought to her on a tray by one of the kitchen staff.

To her surprise, when she then shook hands with Sir Richard, he raised her hand to his lips and greeted her,

"You look even more beautiful in daylight than you did last night."

Because Sheila could not think of a suitable answer, she merely smiled at him.

Again to her surprise she found, as he led the way into the dining room, that there were no other guests other than herself and the Viscount.

As if he read her thoughts, Sir Richard said,

"I am being selfish today. If I had a party, I would undoubtedly have had to talk a lot of nonsense to women, who were only thinking about themselves or men who had never aspired to explore anything further than their Club's betting book!"

The Viscount laughed.

"We cannot all be like you, Richard. I know the real reason you have brought me here today is because you want me to invest in one of your sensational searches for either weapons that have been buried deep in the ground for thousands of years or perhaps the bones of those who fought with them."

Sir Richard laughed.

"That is quite right, Charles, and you are certainly quicker brained than you used to be, which is meant as a compliment!"

"A somewhat backhanded one I might think," the Viscount replied. "But you must tell me all about it and, for goodness sake, let's order our luncheon first or Miss Ash and I will starve."

"I will not allow you to do that," he answered.

They sat in a window seat that had a stunning view of the Thames.

Sheila thought that it looked even more enchanting than it had been when they drove beside it.

"Where are you off to now?" the Viscount asked Sir Richard when they had ordered what sounded to Sheila like three delicious dishes.

"I am very anxious," Sir Richard replied, "to go to the land that is North of Tibet where I am told there was once a large fortification, but which has not been looked at, or should I say discovered, for many years."

The Viscount sat back in his seat.

"Trust you, Richard, to find somewhere that is not only unknown but also extremely uncomfortable. If you are suggesting to me that I should join you, the answer is 'no', before we go any further."

"I can well do without your company," Sir Richard replied. "But then what I really want is your approval and encouragement."

The Viscount looked at him in surprise.

"What do you mean by that?" he asked.

"You have a most important name," Sir Richard answered, "and, if you show you are interested, a number of men as influential as yourself will do the same."

He paused before he went on,

"That is what I need at the moment, encouragement from the top rather than have to work my way up from the bottom."

The Viscount grinned.

"That is very nicely put and, of course, I will help you where I can. If you want to hold meetings to impress those who will listen to you, my house is always at your disposal."

"That is exactly what I would want," Sir Richard said, "and thank you so much for being so understanding. I have struck a bad period at the moment where people are not really interested in the world they do not know, which to me is always implicitly exciting."

"I know," the Viscount replied, "and, of course, I will help you. If it is just a question of sending out letters, Miss Ash can do them. If they are written on my writing paper, the receiver will be aware that I am involved as far as that at any rate."

"You are saying exactly what I wanted you to say," Sir Richard enthused, "and I cannot tell you how grateful I am."

At that very moment a man came up to speak to the Viscount and Sir Richard turned towards Sheila.

"Do tell me more," she begged him. "I am very interested in what you are saying and, of course, you will have to write a book about your different explorations so that we can all appreciate your achievements."

"I have already thought of doing so," Sir Richard replied.

He turned as he spoke towards the Viscount on his other side.

As he did so, Sheila could hear what the stranger who had interrupted them was saying to the Viscount.

"I am delighted to find you here today, my Lord," he said, "because I am issuing an invitation that I know you will accept because it is something entirely up your street."

"What is it?" the Viscount asked him.

"I have just rented, so that I will have a house in the country, one of the finest in the whole of England. What it has, which makes it different from most of the others, is a Racecourse."

"I am wondering which one it could possibly be," the Viscount declared.

Without being asked the man pulled up a chair from the empty table next door and sat down.

"It is Rosswood Hall," the stranger said. "It was going to rack and ruin until its present owner took over. He is now polishing things up a bit now and I am helping him because I want the use of his Racecourse."

Sheila drew in her breath.

She could hardly believe what she was hearing.

But the stranger went on,

"It is full of all the pictures and other things which people make a fuss about. I know you, my dear Viscount, of all people will enjoy the Racecourse."

He hesitated for a moment before he added,

"What I am now arranging next week is a kind of introduction to my new country home. It will be a special steeplechase and a flat race and you can bring your own horses to it."

He saw the Viscount was looking interested and he continued,

"You, for instance, could bring two of your best horses, one for jumping and the other the fastest on the flat. I am asking twelve other men who have the same sort of horses as you have to compete with you and to challenge you."

"I call it a splendid idea," the Viscount said. "It ought to be very amusing for us all."

"I rather thought that was how you would feel," the stranger said. "I promise you it will be not only exciting to take part but also to watch it. I have some very charming people coming down including many of your friends."

He smiled as he concluded,

"It will be a send-off for my country seat which no one else has thought of."

"I think it is a new and unusual idea," the Viscount agreed. "What do you think Richard? By the way I have not introduced you yet. This is Mr. Angus McLever. He comes, I understand, from the very North of Scotland and is ready to entertain us here in the South."

"I will certainly try and I will expect you, once I have put it into a decent shape, to enjoy the house I have rented, my Lord," Angus McLever then added. "It certainly holds a number of treasures inside that should please you when you are not riding."

"Let me appraise you, Angus, of my friend who is the best explorer in the country," the Viscount said. "It will do him good to explore at home instead of having to go a million miles to find what he desires!"

Angus McLever held out his hand and Sir Richard took it.

"Now let me introduce Miss Ash."

The Scotsman bowed a little coldly to Sheila and turned back to the two men.

"I want both of you to come down this weekend," he told them. "Then you can advise me about what steps I should take after that. It is going to be very exciting and, of course, my dear Viscount, you must bring your two best horses. I will be very disappointed if they don't win both races."

"I will be perfectly happy to lose the jumping one," the Viscount replied, "because my horse is still young and has not had a great deal of experience. But it is certainly an original idea of yours."

"I would hope to give you a great many more in the future," Angus McLever said. "And I have never seen a house with more beautiful contents and I have seen quite a number."

Sheila was listening feeling almost paralysed.

How was it possible that her cousin could have let The Hall so quickly?

She could only pray that he had made arrangements for Wilkins and his wife and, of course, her dogs who were with them.

It seemed so extraordinary to her that he should do something that had never been done before by any of her ancestors in all the centuries in letting the family house out to strangers.

She could not help thinking that it was an appalling thing to have done without the Earl telling her about his intentions.

She could only wonder why Wilkins had not told her about this new development.

Angus McLever was still insisting that the Viscount came to stay the following weekend.

He then moved back to another table where there were three men talking to each other.

From the look of them, Sheila thought, they were rather rough and certainly not gentlemen.

After Angus McLever had left them, the Viscount said,

"I enjoy original ideas as much as you do, Richard. I will certainly enjoy racing my own horses against those of my friends."

"All the same I should be careful of that man," Sir Richard warned.

"Why would you say that?" the Viscount enquired. "What is wrong with him?"

"I don't know," Sir Richard replied. "But I have a feeling that he is not what he appears to be."

Listening to him Sheila was thinking very much the same.

There had been something not quite right about the way he had talked about her home.

She could not put it into words even to herself.

Yet the feeling was there that this idea of getting all the young men together with their pet horses was not just the amusement they would expect it to be, but something else.

'I don't know why I feel like this,' she mused to herself.

They enjoyed a delicious luncheon.

When he was driving her home, the Viscount talked excitedly of what he would do to win the steeplechase if not the flat race.

"It has certainly given us something very different to think about," he said.

"What do you usually think about?" Sheila asked the Viscount rather abruptly.

It was just a question that came into her mind.

But to her surprise the Viscount looked away as if it was a question he did not wish to answer.

And because she was curious, Sheila could not help pressing him,

"So have you heard of Rosswood Hall before, my Lord?"

"Of course I have heard of it," the Viscount replied, "although I have never been there. I am told its pictures are fascinating, but someone, although I cannot remember who, told me the place has been very neglected."

"I expect the last owner did not have enough money to keep it as it should be," Sheila remarked.

She thought as she spoke how her father had tried so hard to gain the money he needed and she knew that he would have spent it all on his house and his estate.

It would never have occurred to him to give smart parties in London or balls which would have introduced her into the Social world.

It had been her mother who had thought of those possibilities.

But now they were both, she prayed, in Heaven.

All that was left of her home had now gone to this odd Scotsman who would perhaps bring it back in some way to how it had been in the past.

"You are now looking worried and rather sad," the Viscount said unexpectedly.

Sheila smiled.

"Not really," she replied. "I was just wondering if there would be a lot of work waiting for me when I go back to the house."

"Oh, bother the work," the Viscount answered her, "it can look after itself, while I must look to my horses."

He paused for a moment before he went on,

"He might have asked you to the party too. After all, if Richard and I are to be his guests, it would have been polite to have invited you as you were with us."

"I have a feeling." Sheila said, "it will be men only entertainment."

"Yes, of course, that is true. He did not mention his other guests and as you say perhaps it is entirely a sporting effort and the ladies would be bored."

She reflected that anything to do with horses would never bore her, but she thought it a mistake to say so.

It would look as if she was asking him to get her an invitation to the party and that was the last thing she should do.

'I must remember,' she told herself, 'that I am just a secretary. Although he has so been kind to me because I saved him from being thirteen at table the other night, there is no reason why he should have brought me to that lovely luncheon with Sir Richard.'

She paused for a moment as she worked it out in her mind and then said to herself,

'He could easily have said that I would not be in London this week, but with my family elsewhere. But, of course, Sir Richard has no idea that I am only the hired help in the Viscount's home.'

It was a somewhat depressing thought.

At that moment they drew up outside the house in Park Lane.

"Thank you very much indeed for taking me out to luncheon with Sir Richard, my Lord," Sheila said. "I have enjoyed every moment of it and it was very very kind of you."

"It was kind of you to come with me," the Viscount answered, "and now I suppose we have to cope with those tiresome letters asking me to something I invariably don't want to go to."

Sheila laughed.

"I will attempt to make you sound as though you are sacrificing your amusements for something much more important."

As the carriage came to a standstill and a footman opened the door, she stepped out.

The Viscount stopped to give some instructions to the groom.

By the time he had turned towards the door, she had disappeared.

She was in fact up in her room taking off her finery and putting on the simple dress she usually wore when she was working.

Almost instinctively she walked to the window to look out at the sunshine.

She was thinking how lovely it would be at The Hall and the sun would now be shining on the lake and the garden.

She had always felt that because it was her home and had been in the family for so many generations, things would never alter.

The house might get shabby and run down, but it would still be itself and it would still belong, as it always had, to the Rosswoods.

But now a stranger had walked in and taken it over.

Maybe he would now change everything to his own liking, which would be very different from the way it had been in the past.

She was also worrying about Wilkins and his wife.

Supposing the new occupier did not think that they were good enough and then sent them away.

'I must find out where they are and what is now happening,' Sheila thought frantically.

Because she was so frightened that she might lose them and that would be disastrous, she ran downstairs to her office and started to write to Wilkins.

She told him about how she had met a Scotsman at luncheon and he had said that he was having a large party next weekend to which everyone would bring their horses.

"*I am worrying about you and Mrs. Wilkins,*" she wrote. "*I would hope that the Scotsman has given you enough help to run the house properly as you have always wanted it to be.*

At the same time it has been with the Rosswoods for centuries and I find myself resenting the fact that he is now in command and things will never be the same as they were in the past.

Please, please write to me at once and tell me what is happening.

You know how much you both mean to me and I am so worried you might find this new owner unbearable."

As she wrote this, she was much more frightened that the Scotsman might want to bring in his own servants and think that Wilkins and his wife were too old.

'If they are turned away, what can I do?' she asked herself.

It seemed to her that for the moment she was under a dark cloud and she could not find a way out.

*

The next day and the day after she waited anxiously for a letter from Wilkins.

When it came, it was brought with the other letters to her office by one of the footmen.

As she took it in both her hands, she knew for the moment that she was almost too scared to open it.

She feared it might carry the bad news which she was powerless to alter.

Then she pulled out of the envelope a letter written on a piece of headed writing paper.

For a while Wilkins's rather untidy writing seemed to swim in front of her eyes.

Then she read,

"*My Lady,*

Don't worry, things have changed as you say and his Lordship's gone back to where he came from.

"*He's let the house for what I understand be a very big sum and the workmen be busy all day doing it up.*

The Missus now has two people to help her in the kitchen and I has two footmen, so things be better than I expected, but I only wish that your Ladyship were here with us.

Please don't worry,

Yours sincerely

Wilkins."

Sheila gave a sigh of relief.

She need not have been so frightened.

Of course, as her cousin was very well off, he could afford to take on extra servants in the house.

But she never dreamt that he would rent it out.

However, if it brought in the money that was badly needed for the repairs and improvements, then it had been a wise thing to do, although such an idea had never entered her father's head.

'He would have found it impossible,' she thought, 'and so would Mama, to have let strangers take over their home and alter it however necessary it was.'

Now that her cousin had gone back to where he came from she must carry on trying to live her own life and support herself.

Three days later she had a letter from Sir Richard thanking her for the letter she had written to him, thanking him for the delightful luncheon at *The Grand Hotel.*

He told her he was going North to see a certain museum in Edinburgh as they were particularly interested in what he had acquired on his last journey abroad.

"*When I come back*," he wrote, "*you must lunch with me again.*

I do want to tell you more about my last discovery which was very unusual.

I think I should warn you about the man who is talking to Charles about his Racecourse.

I don't know much about him, but I am certain that he is not the Scotsman he says he is.

I may be wrong, but I would not mind betting I am right and we must talk about it when we meet.

But until we do keep an eye on Charles and see that he does not get caught by one of those slick talkers.

Although I may be exaggerating, I have a feeling that the Scotsman is one of them.

Your friend,

Richard."

Sheila read the letter several times.

It struck her as being very odd that she should have felt almost the same, although she had not actually put it into words.

There had been something about the man and the way he rushed at the Viscount that made her suspect that it was not just friendliness.

He had some other reason for being so effusive to him.

'I wonder what it is?' she asked herself.

But the Viscount seemed to have disappeared and, as she had no idea what went on in the other parts of the house, he was obviously keeping himself to himself as the servants would say.

But she had no one to discuss it with or to answer any questions she might put to them.

As it happened she had very little time to think of anything but the work she was doing.

The servants had to be paid and there were endless bills for food and champagne and, if the Viscount was not entertaining, Rupert was certainly thrilled to be free and back with his friends.

They were much younger than his brother and very much noisier, but they certainly enjoyed themselves.

Almost every day of the week there were young people to luncheon or dinner and parties in the evening, which went on until the early hours of the morning.

'At least he is wise to celebrate his freedom with his friends,' Sheila thought.

She was very touched with the flowers Rupert gave her when inadvertently Bates had told him that it was her birthday.

She also had a cake from the cook and a card from Wilkins and his wife.

'At least they have not forgotten me,' she thought to herself.

She wished that she could celebrate her birthday by going to the theatre, but she was too shy and perhaps too wise to go alone.

There was no one she could ask to accompany her.

She was actually feeling just a little hurt that since the luncheon party at *The Grand Hotel* she had hardly set eyes on the Viscount.

He had sent her the letters that needed answering by one of the servants, who collected them in the evening for him to sign before they were posted.

She wondered if she had offended him in any way or maybe he was behaving as any normal gentleman would behave to the family secretary who was of no particular significance.

At the same time she wanted to see him.

She liked him and there was indeed something very likeable about him.

Also she could not help admiring him.

And she could easily understand why women like the Countess pursued him.

When she went to bed, she often wondered if they were together.

And if the Countess was still making it quite clear to everyone that he belonged to her.

It gave her a little ache in her heart when she then thought that he was perhaps deliberately avoiding her.

Perhaps he had thought her rather pushy and so was showing her what was her proper place in the house.

It was certainly not in the drawing room, that was for certain.

'I must not think about it,' Sheila said to herself. 'This is the life I have to live and I must get used to being thrown on one side when I am no longer useful and quite obviously easily forgotten about.'

It was one thing to think about it.

But quite another to be able to stop the strange pain in her heart because she had just for once been herself.

She looked at the pretty pink and blue gown she had worn the night she had gone down to dinner.

She thought it very unlikely that she would ever wear it again.

In fact, as far as she was concerned, the Viscount had vanished.

She was certain that in the future he would make sure that they were not unexpectedly thirteen at dinner.

'Why must I keep thinking about him?' she asked the stars as she stood at the window before getting into her bed.

She looked up at the sky as she pleaded,

'I want to think of Rosswood Hall and step back in time to hear my Papa coming in through the front door and Mama coming out of the drawing room to kiss him. Why, why is all that in the past? What is there for me in the future?'

There was no answer from the sky.

When she then drew the curtains over the windows to shut out the stars, there were tears in her eyes.

CHAPTER SEVEN

On the Sunday morning Sheila woke up early.

She lay in bed thinking that today at any rate she need not go to the office.

She decided that she would start the day correctly by going to Church as she always had with her mother.

They had gone to St. George's in Hanover Square. She loved the Church and had always enjoyed the beautiful singing of the choir.

She felt that it would take away all her constant thoughts that kept roaming towards the Viscount, however much she tried to think of other things.

All day yesterday she had wondered how he was doing with the racing on the Racecourse she knew only too well.

She felt that Angus McLever had had it cleared out and made perfect before he invited his guests to race their horses and take the jumps her father had carefully erected.

'I would have loved to see them racing yesterday,' she kept thinking.

At the same time it would have been sad for her to go back and see her old home beginning to look as it had when she was a child.

Of course Angus McLever would have spent some of his enormous fortune on making it as impressive as it had been originally.

It would take time to do what had to be done and even if he had put six gardeners at work it was doubtful if it would look as glorious as it had been in her grandfather's day.

She tried to be grateful that the new Earl had let the house to someone so rich.

Even though, to all intents and purposes, her home now belonged to a stranger.

She had told the maids not to wake her and it was nine o'clock before she finally climbed out of bed and put on one of her prettiest dresses to go to Church.

She was just thinking that she would go downstairs and ask them to give her some breakfast, when there was a knock on the door.

"Come in," she called out.

She thought that it was one of the maids who was always very helpful to her.

To her surprise it was one of the footmen.

"His Lordship wants to see you in the study, Miss Ash," he said.

Sheila looked at him in astonishment.

"Is his Lordship back?" she asked.

"Yes, he is," the footman replied. "He comes back home about an hour ago and has had his breakfast and now wants to see you."

Sheila thought it a good thing that she was dressed and responded,

"I will come down to him at once. Thank you very much, Tom."

As she went downstairs, she wondered why he had left Rosswood Hall so early. Indeed he must have left very soon after daybreak to be home by now.

'I wonder what has happened,' she kept saying in her mind until she opened the door of the study.

As she did so, there was a yelp and Dickie, her labrador, who was sitting by the Viscount's feet rushed towards her.

She put her arms round him and hugged him.

The dog was obviously very excited at seeing her and jumped about barking and wagging its tail.

Having hugged him, she put him down and walked towards the Viscount.

He rose from the writing table where he had been sitting and said,

"The butler at Rosswood Hall, whose name I think is Wilkins, told me that this dog has been pining at having lost you and made me bring him back with me. And by the way your other dog, Teal, has apparently settled down very well in the kitchen."

"How kind of you," Sheila cried. "Of course I am thrilled to have him if you don't mind him in the house."

"I cannot understand," the Viscount said, "why did you not tell me that you had worked at Rosswood Hall."

Sheila, having no wish to answer this question, then patted Dickie before she replied,

"Thank you very much for bringing him back to me, my Lord. I was afraid he would be unhappy without me and I missed him every day."

"Why did you not tell me? Of course I would have allowed you to bring him here."

Sheila gave a deep sigh.

"How could I have known that anyone would have been so considerate as to let me have a dog when I was just a secretary? I promise you he will be very good and will be no trouble to anyone."

There was a pause.

Then the Viscount said in a rather strangled voice,

"I need your help."

"My help!" she exclaimed. "What has happened? But first do tell me, my Lord, did you win yesterday?"

"I won both races," the Viscount said sharply as if he was not that interested in the racing yesterday and did not wish to talk about it.

"How splendid!" Sheila enthused. "I thought that you would and you must feel very proud."

"Actually," the Viscount replied, "I am feeling very worried and I need your help. Sit down, Miss Ash, and I will tell you what has happened."

He spoke in such an odd way that Sheila looked at him questioningly, but she did not say anything.

She had learnt of old that it was best for people who had something to tell you to talk first so that every detail of what was worrying them could be properly analysed.

She wondered, however, what could have occurred.

She hoped that it was nothing to do with her home or Wilkins and Mrs. Wilkins.

The Viscount was looking down at his blotter and fiddling with a pen.

There was an ominous pause until at last he said,

"I am in trouble, *desperate* trouble! As you have been so wonderful in saving Rupert, I must ask you now to save me."

"To save you?" she echoed in astonishment. "What has happened, my Lord? What have you done?"

The Viscount took a deep breath.

Then he said,

"As you know, Mr. McLever, who gave the party, was extremely anxious for me to be present at it. In fact I thought, even when we were in the hotel, he rather over-emphasised his invitation and seemed somehow afraid that I might refuse."

Sheila thought that this needed no comment and was therefore silent.

"When I arrived," the Viscount went on, "I found to my surprise that no women had been asked to the party. His daughter, Ursula, was the only female present."

He paused, but, as Sheila said nothing because she was wondering how this was such a problem, he went on,

"As most of the other riders were either friends of mine or men I knew, I was delighted to see them. The first night we had an excellent, but somewhat rowdy dinner party. Ursula sat on my right, which I quite understood. I am afraid I said very little to her during the meal for the simple reason there was so much noise and joking among my friends that I hardly noticed her at all."

Sheila was thinking of the big dining room at The Hall, which she had always thought was one of the most enchanting rooms in the house.

How lovely it had been when there were flowers on the table as well as the magnificent engraved candlesticks that her father had sold.

"When the one lady left the room," the Viscount continued, "I am afraid the conversation became somewhat bawdy and it was a good thing that there were no females present."

"I would suppose that after dinner you went to the music room," Sheila said unthinkingly.

She recalled that this was what they had usually done when there had been a party given by her mother.

"Yes, we certainly did," the Viscount agreed. "You must know, as you have worked there, that it is the most attractive room in the house. I appreciated the music that came from such a magnificent piano as fortunately one of my friends is an acknowledged pianist."

Sheila made no comment and after a moment the Viscount continued,

"The next day the races took place. We were all in tremendous good spirits when we went back to The Hall. I was particularly delighted that both my horses had shown themselves to be unbeatable and my friends teased me at being conceited about them."

Sheila felt that she could almost hear them laughing and talking and enjoying themselves just as those who had come to The Hall when she was a child had relished her mother's parties.

"We were late going to bed, as you can imagine," the Viscount went on. "I was actually rather tired."

"Which was not surprising having won both races," Sheila remarked.

To her surprise he went on as if she had not spoken, saying,

"I undressed. Then I went into the bathroom."

He paused and she looked at him quizzically as it seemed as if he found it difficult to go on.

Then, as if he was forcing himself to speak, he said,

"When I came back into my bedroom wearing only my nightshirt, I realised that there was now more light in the room than when I had left it. Then, to my astonishment, I saw – Ursula – *in my bed!*"

His voice seemed almost to break on the name.

Sheila stared at him in amazement.

She wondered where this long story was going to end.

Never for a moment has she imagined anything like this.

"In your bed," she repeated in a whisper.

"In my bed," the Viscount confirmed, "propped up against the pillows. I realised as if someone was telling me so that this was a trap and McLever had been planning it ever since he had arranged the racing."

Sheila drew in her breath.

She had thought when he had talked to them at *The Grand Hotel* that Angus McLever was an unpleasant man.

But she began to recognise that with his enormous fortune he desired a title for his daughter.

"I saw it all in a flash," the Viscount went on, "that the whole thing had been set-up to catch me and force me into matrimony with his daughter."

His voice sharpened as he added,

"If I had any sense, I would have realised from the beginning that being so rich he wanted his only child, who would inherit his money, to have a title. Who has an older or better one than me?"

Again there was silence until Sheila asked in a low voice,

"What did you do?"

"I was just about to tell her to get out of my bed and leave me alone," the Viscount replied, "when the door opened and there was McLever with two witnesses. One man was even making a drawing of me standing by the bed with the girl inside it sitting up against my pillows!"

"It is quite disgraceful of him!" Sheila exclaimed.

"I was quiet for a moment because I could not think of anything to say," the Viscount went on as if she had not spoken. "Then McLever had the nerve to say to me, 'you are behaving disgracefully to my daughter, Stone, and you will marry her as soon as it can be arranged'."

Sheila gave another exclamation, but did not speak.

"I was about to tell him I would do nothing of the sort when he walked away with one of the men beside him. The other man finished his drawing before he left the room and closed the door behind him."

As the story seemed to have come to an end, there was silence.

Then Sheila asked,

"What did you do then, my Lord?"

"I told Ursula to leave immediately," the Viscount answered, "and she went out without saying a word. Then I realised what a fool I had been to accept the invitation of such a man in the first place. Why I had not realised that it was a trap from the moment I arrived, as Ursula was at my side at every meal, I just don't know."

He paused before he added,

"I hardly spoke to her, but her father made it clear to the other men in the party that, as she was at my side, to all intents and purposes she was my possession."

There was another long silence before Sheila said,

"He was very clever in capturing you, but what are you going to do about it?"

"That is why I have turned to you for help," the Viscount replied. "Only *you* can save me."

"You know that I will do anything I possibly can," Sheila answered. "But I just cannot help thinking that it is going to be rather difficult."

"That is exactly what McLever intends," he said miserably. "If I had had any sense in my head, I would have made some excuse to leave the party as soon as I had arrived."

He made a wide gesture with his hands before he continued,

"But, of course, I was thinking of my horses and wanting to show them off. And every man was feeling the same, so it was in fact a great triumph for me to win both races."

"What are you going to do now?" Sheila asked.

"That is what I am asking you. You are the wise one. You thought of how to spirit Rupert away from the Chinese, when I believed that the only way out was to pay them the enormous amount of money they wanted. I can only pray that you will save me now."

"Have you any idea of how I can do so?" Sheila asked.

She was feeling almost helpless, although she was well aware that she had read about the way women, when they had an attractive *debutante* daughter, tried to catch an important title for her by marriage.

A man who did not want to be caught had to be very careful not to pay a girl too much attention or to be alone with her for any length of time.

She had heard from one of her father's friends how Lord Worcester had been caught because he spent some time in the garden talking to a pretty girl.

Her mother said that he had prejudiced her by doing so and she had even asked the Prince of Wales to support her in saying that the only thing Lord Worcester could do to save her reputation was to marry her.

Now she thought about it, it seemed impossible, as Ursula had been seen in his bedroom, for the Viscount to avoid being pressed into marriage against his will.

She was quiet for a moment.

Then she thought that he might disappear by going abroad, as he said again,

"Now you have heard what has happened to me, I am asking you to help."

"How can I do that?" Sheila asked him.

"I am expecting, as I crept out of the house when everyone was asleep, that McLever will follow me here and demand my assurances that I will marry his daughter. I can only think of one way that I can answer him."

"What can that be?"

She was wondering what it could possibly be.

She thought it would be clever of him to think of anything, while for the moment her mind was quite blank.

"When he arrives here," the Viscount said quietly, "I want to introduce you as my fiancée."

Sheila stared at him.

Then she smiled,

"That is very astute of you."

"You mean you will do it?" he asked.

"Yes, of course I will," Sheila replied. "It will be difficult for him to know what to say."

"If you will really help me," he answered, "I think we have the perfect reason to send him away. After all, as my father is so ill, we have not announced our engagement hoping that he would recover before we married."

"Yes, of course. That is very subtle of you. I am sure then that the horrible Mr. McLever will not have any answer to that."

"That is just what I am hoping and praying," the Viscount said, "and thank you, thank you more than I can possibly say for being so helpful."

He put out his hand as he spoke.

Sheila had risen from the seat where she had been sitting and now put her hand into his.

"You are wonderful," he said. "I don't think there could be anyone like you in the whole world."

Because his fingers had closed on hers, Sheila felt a strange feeling in her heart.

She was also very touched by the note of gratitude in his voice.

Then to her surprise he raised her hand to his lips and kissed it.

For the moment it was difficult to breathe.

As she tried to think of something to say, the door opened and Bates announced,

"Mr. Angus McLever, my Lord."

Quickly Sheila took her hand from the Viscount's as he rose to his feet and Angus McLever came into the room.

He looked, Sheila thought, even more unpleasant than she had thought him to be when she last saw him at *The Grand Hotel.*

There was also an expression of satisfaction on his rather coarse and ugly face as if he had won the game and had every intention of crowing over being the victor.

The Viscount made no effort to move towards him.

Angus McLever walked to the centre of the room and said,

"You left very early in the morning, Charles, and did not say goodbye as I expected you to do."

"I had business to see to in London," the Viscount replied slowly and in a very quiet voice.

He took a deep breath before he continued,

"Before we proceed any further, I must introduce you to my fiancée, Miss Alma Ash. We have been engaged for some time, but have not announced it as yet because of my father's prolonged illness."

Angus McLever was stunned into silence.

Then his eyes narrowed as he declared,

"If you think you can get away with that story, you are very much mistaken. You behaved abominably to my daughter and I demand satisfaction."

The Viscount did not speak.

Angus McLever then drew a piece of paper from the pocket of his coat and opened it.

"Here is the picture of you with her in your room," he said. "Unless you agree to marry Ursula, I will give this drawing to the newspapers who will, I am quite sure, make a good story out of it."

Because she was so shocked at what he was saying, Sheila gasped.

As she did so, almost as if Dickie realised what was happening, he growled and moved towards the Scotsman standing in the centre of the room.

As the dog came up him, Angus McLever squealed,

"Take that damn dog away! If there's anything I hate, it's dogs."

He spoke rudely and harshly and, as his voice rang out, Sheila's eyes opened wide.

She then stared at him as if she could hardly believe what she was seeing.

She had thought when she first saw him that there was something strange about him.

Yet she could not remember seeing him before.

But now almost like a flash of lightning, it came to her.

She had heard him speaking in that harsh voice to Dickie when he had come several years ago to Rosswood Hall to see her father.

She had learnt later that he had come to take away from him all that he could from his almost empty bank account.

Then, as Dickie growled at him, as he had done at The Hall, she spoke up and her voice seemed to ring out in the room,

"You are not Angus McLever as you are pretending to be, you are Frederick Smith!"

Almost as if she had shot a bullet at him, the man turned to look at her.

"What do – you mean?" he stammered.

"I mean you were Frederick Smith when you came to Rosswood Hall and took the Earl of Rosswood's money away saying that you had a marvellous scheme for making an enormous amount of money very quickly."

"I wish I did," he snarled.

"Obviously you did or you would not be behaving as you are now, changing your name and trying to marry your daughter into the aristocracy."

"You have no right at all to speak to me like that," Frederick Smith replied sharply. "If I have changed my name as I have by Deed Poll it's perfectly legal and, if I've rented Rosswood Hall, then it's no business of yours as its owner is now dead."

"It's owner is dead," Sheila told him, "but he had a family and therefore his money, which you stole from him, should have been given to those following him."

"He had no son," Frederick Smith snapped, "and anyway it's none of your business."

"Unfortunately for you it is *my* money you have stolen in such a disgraceful way," Sheila shouted angrily, "and I demand here and now that you give it to me."

Frederick Smith's eyes widened and he stared at her in astonishment before he said unpleasantly,

"Who the devil are you?"

"The man you were defrauding was my father," she answered him. "I am Lady Sheila Rosswood and I demand that you give me all the money you made from my father's investment of fifteen thousand pounds which, judging by what has been said, is now worth many times that amount."

There was silence for a moment before Frederick Smith said angrily,

"I don't believe what you are saying. I was told when I arrived that his Lordship was with his secretary."

It was then that the Viscount, who had been quietly listening to this exchange of words in disbelief, spoke up,

"I am completely certain of one thing," he said, "and that is that Lady Sheila is telling the truth while you are lying. Unless the money which you received from his Lordship is paid immediately, I will inform my Solicitors of your theft."

He paused for a moment before he went on,

"If we go to the Law, it will doubtless ruin your reputation in the Social world, on which, at the moment, you seem to have made quite an impression."

Frederick Smith could not deny this.

He therefore stood looking at them both sullenly as if he wished that he had the power to destroy them.

As if he felt that he had lost the battle, but must somehow save himself from being completely crushed, he said,

"Very well, I will pay Lady Sheila exactly what her father would have received if he had lived. But I will only do so if nothing is said to anyone of what has occurred this morning."

"If you behave with dignity," the Viscount replied, "I promise you that no one will know what has happened between these four walls. Or else as I have already told you, my Solicitors will take up the fight."

He looked at Sheila before he added,

"The Press will certainly glory in it all, especially in the clever way you have managed to defraud the Social elite by pretending to be one of them when, according to Lady Sheila, you are merely out of the gutter!"

Frederick Smith winced at the Viscount's words.

Then, as if he now realised that he was completely defeated, he walked slowly towards the door.

Sheila and the Viscount stood still until he reached it.

Then, as he turned round, the Viscount said,

"No tricks now, Smith, and I give you my word, as I know her Ladyship does, that we will speak to no one of what has occurred either at Rosswood Hall or here in this room."

Frederick Smith drew in his breath.

For a moment Sheila thought that he was going to swear at them.

Then he went through the door slamming it behind him.

Sheila could only stare at the door as if she could hardly believe that they had won an impossible battle.

Then to her astonishment, the Viscount's arms went round her as he asked,

"Why did you not tell me, my darling?"

As he spoke, his lips came down on hers.

She knew that this was what she had been longing for and why she had been feeling so miserable.

She felt as if her heart leapt towards his heart.

As he drew her closer and still closer to him, his lips became more demanding.

She knew that she had found the love that she had longed for that had made her father and mother so happy together.

'I love you, I love you,' she wanted to shout out.

Then she thought that maybe the Viscount was only thanking her for saving him from Ursula and was not really thinking of her.

As he took his lips from hers and she hid her face against his shoulder, he said,

"I have loved you, darling, from the first moment I saw you. But I was afraid, desperately afraid, my family would make a terrible fuss and commotion if I said that I wanted to marry the secretary."

He drew her a little closer as he carried on,

"Now everything is perfect and I want to marry you at once, today or tomorrow, because I just cannot wait any longer."

Sheila raised her head.

"I just don't believe what you are telling me," she sighed.

"I have loved you from the very first," the Viscount murmured. "But I decided I must wait to find some way of making you mine without there being a fuss about it."

"I thought that you had forgotten about me this last week," Sheila smiled.

"It has been agony," the Viscount told her, "not to talk to you and not to see you. But I have been with Papa, as he has been better these last few days than he has been for some time."

He paused before he added,

"I thought in some way it would make me forget you for a short while if I was riding in the races."

"You wanted to forget me?" Sheila asked him.

"It was something I could never do," he replied. "I knew when you were clever enough to snatch Rupert out of the hands of the Chinamen that you were so very different from any woman I have met before. It was just impossible for me to find any woman attractive when I compared them with you."

Sheila gave a little gasp.

She was thinking of the Countess as she asked him,

"Is that really true?"

"I swear to you before God," he answered, "I have lain awake every night wanting you, yearning for you and knowing that in some strange way I could not understand I had found the real love that has always eluded me."

His arms tightened round her as he admitted,

"So many people have tried to marry me to their daughters for my title. And I was a fool not to realise that Angus McLever was doing the same thing."

He hesitated for a moment before he said as if he had just thought of it,

"Is that unique house really your home?"

"It has been mine ever since I was born," Sheila replied, "but Papa, as you doubtless know, gambled away every penny he possessed."

She smiled as she reflected,

"He would have been so thrilled now if he had known that his last hopeless effort at being a millionaire had been successful and it is so sad that he is not here to celebrate it."

"I think he will know," the Viscount said quietly. "Wherever he is, he will be very glad that in the future I will look after you and that there will be no more Frederick Smiths or Angus McLevers taking our money away. I will promise you that."

"But, if I have some money," Sheila said, "and it has been terrible these last few years not being able to give people what they deserved, I will be very careful with it. At least I will be able to help those who have helped me."

She was thinking about Wilkins and Mrs. Wilkins as she spoke.

She thought that she ought to tell the Viscount how wonderful they had been to her.

'It is due to him sending me Dickie,' she thought, 'that made me remember where I had seen Frederick Smith before. How can I ever repay him for that?'

"You are not thinking of me," the Viscount said to her drawing her a little closer.

"Actually I am thinking of the people who were so kind to me when I did not have a penny to my name," she replied. "Now I can pay them all back and tell them how grateful I have been, most of all because I found you."

"Do you really love me just as I am, my darling?" the Viscount asked.

"I was feeling very shy this morning because I was so anxious to see you again. I was thinking of you all day yesterday and was quite certain that you would win."

"I love you and I adore you, Sheila," the Viscount replied, "and we will be very happy. Do you want a big Wedding?"

"No, of course not," Sheila murmured. "It will be much too embarrassing. The best thing we can do is to get married without anyone being aware of it. Therefore no one is likely to connect Lady Sheila with Miss Ash."

"To me they are one and the same person, but you are quite right, my darling, it would not be right to have a big Wedding while Papa is so ill, although actually I was told when I arrived today that he is better than he has been for a long time."

"That is wonderful!" she exclaimed. "Everything is going right for us, I would hate you to go away if your father was near death as they have said ever since I came here."

"Well, they think now that he will recover and after all he is only just a little over seventy so he may live for a long time."

"If your father is well and Rupert will not get into any more difficulties, perhaps we can then have just a tiny little – honeymoon," Sheila whispered.

"We will have a honeymoon when I can tell you over and over again how much I love and adore you," he answered. "As you say, my darling one, because you are always thinking of other people rather than yourself, we will not go far. In fact we will go to France and then we can come back very quickly if necessary."

"I would love to go to France with you, Charles. I answered quite a lot of letters from my Papa when he was gambling on some new ideas in France, which as you know came to nothing and he lost his money."

"We can spend some of his money in enjoying the French countryside," the Viscount replied. "I have no wish for you, darling Sheila, to be thinking of theatres or other amusements when you should be thinking of me!"

"I will always be thinking of you," she whispered. "I thought as soon as I saw you that you were the most handsome man I have ever seen."

"I thought you were the loveliest and most adorable woman I have ever imagined," the Viscount answered. "In fact since the first moment I saw you I have not been able to look at another woman."

"I will make sure," Sheila murmured, "that you will never look at one again!"

The Viscount laughed.

"You are quite safe," he said, "you are betting this time on a certainty."

"Oh, darling, it is so wonderful to know that I need not go on working as a secretary, At the same time I am so grateful to have done so because then I met you."

She thought as she spoke that, although she loved being at her home, nothing could be more marvellous than when she had a home of her own with the Viscount.

As if he knew what she was thinking, he said,

"There is one thing you have not seen which you are going to see almost immediately and that is our house in the country."

"I did not know you had one," Sheila answered.

"Of course we have one," the Viscount told her. It has been in the family for hundreds of years and, although it is not as large as Rosswood Hall, it is still, I think, one of the most beautiful Elizabethan houses in existence."

"Why did you not tell me about it before?" Sheila enquired.

"Because it has been shut up ever since my father became so ill and had to be in London so that he was near to the best doctors," the Viscount replied. "But I am sure he will understand that I want to open it up now that I am to be married. We will have our horses and, of course, our dogs there."

"It was really Dickie who saved us," Sheila told him. "I think he recognised Frederick Smith as soon as he came into the room. When he cursed him as he cursed him the first time he came to Rosswood Hall, I knew that he was indeed a horrible man, who would deceive Papa as he had been deceived so often before."

"You must remember that he won *this* gamble," the Viscount said, "and, if he has made as much as he always boasted he had, people will accuse me of marrying you for your money."

Sheila laughed.

"They are much more likely to say I am marrying you for your title."

"We are marrying each other because I have been searching for you ever since I grew up and found out that women were attractive."

"I have always believed that my prayers would be answered," Sheila sighed, "and that someday, somehow, somewhere I would find you."

"On top of everything else you have solved all my problems for me, my darling glorious Sheila, firstly with the Chinaman and then with Frederick Smith."

"Not me, my dearest Charles," she replied. "It was love that solved all the problems and will keep us blissfully happy for the rest of our lives and all the lives we have yet to live together."

Then, as the Viscount's lips made hers captive and he drew her closer and still closer to him, she knew that they had together found real love, the love that comes from God and is part of God and would be theirs for all Eternity.